TO LOVE AND PERISH

Borgo Press Books by Ernest Dudley

The Amazing Martin Brett: Classic Crime Stories
Department of Spooks: Stories of Suspense and Mystery
More Cases of a Private Eye: Classic Crime Stories
The Private Eye: Classic Crime Stories
The Return of Sherlock Holmes: A Classic Crime Tale
To Love and Perish: A Classic Crime Novel

THE DR. MORELLE CLASSIC CRIME SERIES

Dr. Morelle and the Doll: A Classic Crime Novel
Dr. Morelle at Midnight: A Classic Crime Novel
Dr. Morelle Investigates: Two Classic Crime Tales
Dr. Morelle Meets Murder: Classic Crime Stories
The Mind of Dr. Morelle: A Classic Crime Novel
New Cases for Dr. Morelle: Classic Crime Stories

TO LOVE AND PERISH

A CLASSIC CRIME NOVEL

ERNEST DUDLEY

THE BORGO PRESS

MMXIII

TO LOVE AND PERISH

FIRST BORGO PRESS EDITION

Published by Wildside Press LLC

www.wildsidebooks.com

DEDICATION

To the Memory of Jane Grahame

CONTENTS

CHAPTER ONE

The woman half-sitting up in bed could see the rooftops of the houses about half-a-mile away on the other side of Castlebay. The slated roofs of the town huddled down in the valley against the side of the estuary glinted in the sunlight of that dying winter evening of 1955.

There had been a drizzle of sleet earlier, but it had cleared. The banked clouds had shifted beyond the town and out to sea. Now the evening sky was a washed-out blue in the dusk that seeped into the house from the garden.

Ellen Merrill heard a movement next door. Ever since the beginning of her illness her husband had moved into the next room. She had insisted on it. It was essential, she had said, that he got his proper sleep; after all, he still had his work to do. No point in him becoming tired and perhaps falling ill himself.

Dick Merrill was nearly six feet in height, slim and with blond wavy hair, and with features almost classically chiselled, with a short nose, and a smallish mouth. If there was a weakness to be seen in the curl of his lower lip, it was more than balanced by the strength of his jaw. Perhaps his only bad feature were the slightly protuberant eyes which were a bright blue. His eyelashes were dark, and thick. The war had interrupted his job as an accountant which he had just started with a London firm after having become qualified. The end of the war left him the way it had left a few million others, restless and unable to pick up the threads. For a couple of years he had got by on his gratuity, dabbling in the motor business, not very successfully.

And then he had met Ellen Carslake. Her father had left her around £10,000 when he had died a couple of years before. Carslake had been a widower and she was the only child. She had gone overboard for Merrill at first sight.

Ellen Merrill glanced at the clock beside her even as she heard footsteps outside her door; it was Dick coming to give her the medicine which Dr. Griffiths had prescribed her. Her thoughts turned to Dr. Griffiths who had left her with his usual quiet smile and nods of encouragement. But she recalled again what she had thought at the time; had there been a shadow of baffled anxiety in his eyes which she had not noticed before? Or was it her imagination playing tricks on her?

She sighed gently. Her imagination was working overtime lately, but the thought nagged at her again. Was Dr. Griffiths worried about her? Was the illness which had lasted so interminably too much for him? Or for any other doctor? A cold feeling held her. And then she was comforted by the recollection that though once or twice when her husband had suggested calling in someone else, he had later agreed with her not to do so. She took it to mean that her illness wasn't causing him that much concern, after all, that he felt confident that Dr. Griffiths would get her well.

Her mind circled around Dr. Griffiths, a short chunky man who had once been dark, but whose hair was now grey and receding from a round forehead. His father before him had been a doctor, the good old-fashioned kind, but Griffiths was pretty well up with the times. What had been good enough for his old man wasn't necessarily good enough for him. Perhaps one reason for his attitude was that he'd travelled quite a bit both as a ship's doctor, and during the war when he'd spent some time with the forces in Italy.

It was while he had been abroad that his wife on a visit to some friends in London had been killed in an air-raid. There was a son who'd also followed in his father's footsteps, and after qualifying had also gone to sea as a ship's doctor on the New Zealand run. He had met a New Zealand girl; they had got married, and he'd decided to settle down in Auckland, where he was now practising. He was always inviting his old man to go out there for the fishing, and he'd shown Ellen Merrill some photographs and told her how his son's descriptions of the sport to be had made his mouth water.

'But it's too far,' he used to tell her, 'so I'll have to wait until I can retire. Which'll be never. Like my father before me, I shall die in harness.'

She could hear her husband's footsteps approaching.

She forced herself to sit upright, composed her expression into one less sad and ill, and her eyes travelled round the room.

She had always kept a soft spot in her heart for Castlebay, she had often visited it on holiday with her father. She had been lonely after his death and almost as rootless as Merrill; her earlier associations with Castlebay where she had known happy times gave her the idea that she might be able to settle down there with her husband.

Dick Merrill stood in the doorway and came into the room smiling at her confidently, the medicine glass in his hand. 'Time for a little aperitif, darling.'

She forced herself to smile back at him and took the glass.

'I wouldn't mind taking it,' she said, 'though it is so horrid, if it did me some good.'

He patted her hand and she noticed how the sunburned skin contrasted with her own pale fingers which seemed to have become so bony. 'It's what the doctor ordered,' he said.

She had spoken to Dr. Griffiths about changing the medicine and he'd said he'd give her something different, but it still tasted the same to her. It still seemed to do her no good.

'Knock it back, darling,' he was saying, 'and no heeltaps.'

She drank it up, closing her eyes at the unpleasant taste, and opening them suddenly she found herself staring into his, his gaze fixed on her curiously attentive. At once his mouth curved over his white teeth in a smile.

Her eyes shifted from his to the silver-framed calendar over the fireplace. 1st December. 'Which reminds me. I mustn't forget his cheque.'

She felt rather than saw an eye turn quizzically at her and she wished she had left the thought unspoken. Why did she, she asked herself, remind him however obliquely that she held the purse-strings? Like the business of her settling Dr. Griffiths's bill regularly at the end of the month, as she had done since the beginning of her illness, meticulously sending him her cheque without waiting for his bill.

'I think you must be about the only patient who pays a doctor's bill before they get it,' she heard him say in an amused tone.

He was smiling at her as if she were a child. 'You know Dr. Griffiths never sends bills to anyone,' she said. 'That's why.' He gave her a little shrug. 'I know what you are going to say,' she said.

'I think he's a jolly good chap,' he said. 'But I expect he doesn't do so badly all the same.'

'I know, perhaps it is a bit silly of me, but I always feel doctors' bills should be paid before anything else.'

He admitted that Dr. Griffiths was a bit unbusiness-like, and he reminded her that he had once or twice offered to help him cope with the business side of his practice. He'd been up to the house and seen the shambles of his consulting-room, with its old-fash-ioned desk littered with unanswered correspondence, uncashed cheques mingled with bills and fisherman's catalogues, and other miscellaneous odds and ends indicative of Dr. Griffiths's preoccupation with fishing.

'Got a spot more work to do,' he said. 'I brought some papers back from the office.'

'You're not overdoing it, darling?' she said anxiously. 'We don't want you ill.'

'Of course not, darling,' he said. 'I'm enjoying being so busy—' He broke off and his pale blue eyes fixed themselves on her again. 'Though come to think of it, I wouldn't mind a bit of a holiday. I've been thinking,' he went on, and her heart suddenly contracted; he was about to suggest he should go away for a holiday on his own.

'Yes, darling?' she said.

'I've been thinking,' he said again, 'a week or two in the South of France wouldn't do us any harm.'

'Us?'

'Why, of course,' he said, 'when you're better. Let's hop off for a second honeymoon.'

She smiled up at him gratefully.

He bent and kissed her and she exerted all her strength to raise weak, frail arms about his neck. After a few moments he held her as she lay back amongst the pillows, her breathing a little agitated with the exertion, while he stood staring down at her.

She didn't open her eyes again until she heard him at the door so that his back was towards her, and as he went out of the room Ellen Merrill couldn't see the expression on her husband's face.

CHAPTER TWO

1.

The oncoming headlights came up the hill above Castlebay, and as they swung round the corner they held the white Jaguar parked on the side of the road, so that for a moment two faces glimmered white, close together under the drophead. Then the headlights swept over the Jag and tunnelled their way again through the blackness of overhanging trees, up towards Penybryn, where the river twists down towards the estuary.

'That was Dr. Griffiths' car,' Dick Merrill said. He drew his mouth away from hers, his teeth glistening in the Jag's claustrophobic darkness.

She made no comment. She said she would like a cigarette, and he lit one for her. He lit one for himself, and she let her head fall against his shoulder, while he cupped his hand round her breast.

He heard the rumble of thunder somewhere in the distance, and felt her start as a flicker of lightning sped across the dark sky. He turned and she pressed herself to him, while his other hand moved along her thigh. He caught the mutter of thunder again. This time it sounded nearer, so that he drew his head away to listen to its dying echoes.

'What's the matter?'

He told her it sounded like a storm blowing up.

'I didn't notice,' she said, her voice mocking him, and she pulled his face down to hers again.

He was thinking the evening had been oppressive and he had felt a slight headache coming on, the way his head did ache sometimes when there was thunder about; at least it did lately, the past few months. Then he thought he heard the splash of rain on the hood, and she said, her mouth against his, so that he could feel her teeth smooth and the edges sharp: 'You're not concentrating.'

'I think it's going to rain.' He didn't take his mouth away.

She used the four-letter word she often used, and which always shocked him a little, and drew back from him. She gave him the stub of her cigarette which she had been holding and he threw it into the road, and it arched through the darkness and fell on the bank, a few feet above which the woods ran up the hillside.

From the corner of his eye he knew she was watching him as he took a drag from his own cigarette stub. He exhaled slowly so that the smoke clung on the close air about them, then he aimed his stub into the road.

'What's wrong?' he said.

'You, darling,' she said, 'worrying about the rain when you've got your hand up my skirt.'

He turned to her quickly, staring into the eyes which blinked up at him; he could feel his heart racing as he watched the soft moistness of her mouth and the planes of her face dusky white in the glimmer from the dash-lights.

'You didn't hear it that time,' she said. He looked at her questioningly. 'The thunder,' she said.

'I was thinking of something else.'

She kissed him and clung to him, forcing her body against his. She had on only a thin sweater and tight skirt, which was pushed up to her thighs as she held him, her fingers digging into his back; his sports-jacket was open and her hands reached under it beneath his shoulder blades.

'Now...now...,' she was saying; and it was always this way with her, this devouring urgency. He paused for a moment, while she hung on to him and he reached into the car and took the ignition key out of the dash.

She was smiling at him, her eyes brilliant; and he heard the thunder now, and almost immediately after-wards the trees and the road sprang into blue flickering light. 'You think of everything, don't you, darling?' she said.

He saw that her face was a ghastly pallor in the lightning flash, but her eyes were closed against the sudden brilliance. She did not see the expression on his face as he caught what she said. Then his face was in darkness, and he was thrusting the ignition key into his pocket and helping her up the bank, stumbling into the blackness of the trees, until they reached the patch of grass and they knelt down, locked in each other's arms, and there they lay together.

The rain fell out of a starlit sky on to the two shadows. She smiled up at him deliberately, her face wet.

'We'll get soaked, darling,' he said.

'Don't stop…'

2,

Philip Vane and Dr. Griffiths left the Ford by the side of the road; there was no moon but the stars were brilliant, low in the sky. The thunderstorm had been short and sharp and they had sat it out in the car.

Cautiously they got to the side of the pool. Their eyes had grown used to the darkness so that they hardly needed their electric torches to show them the way through the bushes and over the rocks.

'Some say they can catch fish before a thunderstorm.' Dr. Griffiths was keeping his voice down. 'Some say they do best during a storm; some, after a storm.'

He said that anyway the rain would cause the water to become reoxygenated, and the flies to be beaten down on the surface. And, he said that thundery weather does not appear to affect the rise of the fly, as there is often a big rise of fly when thunder is about; the electric discharge apparently eases the pressure which causes the nymphs, waiting to hatch out, to rise to the surface.

The silence in the darkness was broken only by the sound of the running river as they scrambled down through the trees and hedges towards the open pool where the boss-trout lay.

Philip Vane had spent a holiday at Castlebay in 1950.

He had been getting over a car smash which had killed the girl who had been with him. He had been in love with the girl. It was Dr. Griffiths who had helped him cope with his insomnia. They had become friendly, and most evenings he had spent with Dr. Griffiths at the river up above the town. Vane had been prevented from going back to Castlebay next year because he had been serving a prison sentence.

Now, it was the beginning of July, 1956, Vane had been out since May and he had come to Castlebay again. Dr. Griffiths had been glad to see him, it was as if nothing had happened in the meantime.

'Listen,' Dr. Griffiths was saying, under his breath. Vane heard the soft splash that immediately followed. 'Another damned fisherman.'

'Poachers?'

'Not a human fisherman,' Dr. Griffiths said, 'that was an otter.'

The pool was one of several along this stretch of the river caused by erosion of the banks which the waters had whittled away rushing on their way down to the estuary; and here a mass of rock had jutted out to form a shoulder brushing the river aside. It was only a few yards across the pool towards which they were now heading; it was deep and clear, and under a rocky ledge the boss-trout had its holt.

Dr. Griffiths had the first cast while Vane stood out of range and waited. The silence pressed down on them, only the faintest rustle from the tree tops, and the distant mutter of thunder now somewhere out over the sea beyond Conway. Vane didn't hear Dr. Griffiths's fly settle on the water, although he thought he caught a glimpse of it as it flicked the surface.

The minutes passed, and then there came a sudden flash out of the darkness of the pool. Dr. Griffiths gave a grunt, and then the flash had vanished, and Vane felt sure he could see the rod bending, silhouetted against the stars.

'It's hit,' Dr. Griffiths said, mingled disbelief and excitement in his low tones.

A boss-trout is generally old, Dr. Griffiths had told Vane earlier that evening, often past its prime, who seeks out a holt in some big water which offers him maximum security. Lying in the shadowy recesses, the colour of his body altering to match his surroundings, he takes on a dark, sinister appearance; his massive curved jaw fits his ferocity and cunning. He slides from his holt, a menacing shadow through the night-time water, all set to act with deadly precision, striking and ripping into small trout, salmon fry, even small eels.

For twenty minutes Dr. Griffiths played the trout until gradually its curving shape was held suspended while it thrashed the surface of the pool. Then it was caught in the gaff, and it lay there flapping helplessly on the bank. It was the boss-trout all right; in the light of their torches he looked lean and his great black head ugly and vicious-looking. It must have weighed several pounds; Vane had expected it to be a more massive specimen. But he wasn't prepared for Dr. Griffiths's comment as he bent over it.

He straightened suddenly and looking at Vane, with his dark eyes abstracted in the glow from their torches. 'My God,' he said, under his breath, 'Mrs. Merrill.'

Vane stared at him without knowing what he was talking about, and when he asked him what he meant, Dr. Griffiths brushed it aside, saying it was just something that had occurred to him; it was nothing really, he said.

Later Vane supposed he could have said that he had noticed when they had gone out this night that Dr. Griffiths had appeared a little more thoughtful than usual, but in retrospect it seemed merely that he'd been concerned with the boss-trout.

Dr. Griffiths didn't say anything more about Mrs. Merrill, but Vane could tell he was distracted going back in the car. The thrill of landing the boss-trout seemed to have gone.

Vane remembered afterwards that the white Jag he had noticed in the headlights on their way up to Penybryn was no longer parked by the side of the road. But he didn't connect it with Dr. Griffiths's remark about Mrs. Merrill.

Dr. Griffiths dropped him at the Antelope Inn, where Vane was staying. They said goodbye, Vane was returning to London next day, and Dr. Griffiths went on home. But it wasn't until the dawn crept down the valley that the doctor finally fell asleep, to be woken by his housekeeper an hour and a half later, at his usual time. By then Vane had left for London.

CHAPTER THREE

1.

The telephone rang in Castlebay police station and the desk-sergeant got it. He listened and then he put down the receiver, and went out and across the passage to Inspector Owen's office, and knocked and went in. 'It's Dr. Griffiths, sir,' he said. 'On the phone he is.'

'What about?'

'He didn't say; he didn't want to discuss the matter on the telephone, he said.'

'All right, tell him to look in, anytime this morning. I shall be here.'

The police station was a red-brick building in the middle of one side of Castle Square; at the back a cliff rose up on top of which towered the ruined old castle from which the town took its name. An hour later, as the clock in Castlebay clock-tower in the centre of the square was striking midday, Dr. Griffiths arrived at the police station, and the desk-sergeant showed him into Inspector Owen's room.

Inspector Owen got up from a large oak desk, and pulled out a chair and asked Dr. Griffiths what his visit was in aid of.

'It's difficult,' Dr. Griffiths said slowly, as he faced the other. 'I don't exactly know. The truth is I'm worried about something, and I don't know what to do. Truth to tell, I don't know if I ought to do anything at all.'

Inspector Owen had sat down again in his old, creaking swivel-chair and he leaned forward, his elbows on the desk, his square chin resting on his stubby hands. 'Afraid of disclosing anything that might be regarded as contrary to the ethics of the medical profession and all that?'

'Exactly.'

'Someone going to have a baby who shouldn't?'

'If only it was as simple as that.' Dr. Griffiths shifted uneasily. Then he opened his mouth and let the words come out. 'It concerns Dick Merrill and Mr. Stone,' he said.

'And no doubt Mrs. Stone,' Inspector Owen said slowly. 'Gossip gets around here as quickly as any other small town.'

Dr. Griffiths reflected for a moment or two. Then looking straight at the other he said: 'Look here, the night before last I had a telephone call from Mrs. Stone. Would I come and see her husband. She said he was sick, terribly sick. I went at once. I found him in bed, and his wife said they had both been to dinner with Dick Merrill. Her husband must have eaten something, she thought.'

'Was she sick?'

'No, she was perfectly all right.'

'Had she had the same to eat as her husband?'

Inspector Owen had picked up one of the three pipes that were on his desk, and he got a tin of tobacco out of his desk drawer, pushing his swivel-chair back to rummage for the tin.

Dr. Griffiths nodded. '*Consommé*, roast lamb, and fruit salad and ice cream.'

'Anything special to drink?'

'Just some wine. I think Stone had a brandy as he was leaving.' He paused and then squaring his shoulders, took the plunge. 'That's not the only thing that puzzles me. You know Merrill's wife died about six months ago?' Inspector Owen stopped tapping the tobacco into the bowl of his pipe. 'The symptoms are precisely the same. Only difference is that Mrs. Merrill died and Stone hasn't.'

'From where I'm sitting it sounds as if you're suggesting there's some connection between Mrs. Merrill's death and Mr. Stone's illness.'

'I have no evidence in either case.'

'Evidence of what?'

Dr. Griffiths sat silent, his face set in bitter lines.

Inspector Owen looked at him thoughtfully. 'I know the spot you're in. I want to help you. But for instance, why should Merrill have wanted to get rid of his wife? Or why should he want to get rid of Stone?'

'All I know is that when I was hooking a trout last night, the thought suddenly flashed through my mind that the symptoms in both cases were identical. Now you see why I'm worried. If I make any allegation against Merrill, and it proved to be unfounded it's the end of me. Quite apart from the fact that I'm a friend of his, and I was a friend of his late wife. Fine sort of friend, eh, to start thinking what I'm thinking?'

The other made a sympathetic noise behind his pipe. Dr. Griffiths eyed him anxiously, then drew some comfort from his expression. 'What am I to do?' he said. 'At the same time, if there has been an attempt on Stone's life, mind you I don't say there has been, I don't want there to be another. It might be fatal.'

There was a heavy silence in the office, while the smoke from Owen's pipe drifted lazily in the warm air through the half-open window behind him.

'On what you have told me, I don't see that we can make a move. We've got to have some evidence.'

Dr. Griffiths slowly produced a specimen jar from his pocket. 'That'll tell you whether there's anything in what I have been saying or not.' The other stared at the object on the desk between them. 'I took a sample of Stone's urine. Don't know what made me do it. I suppose I was instinctively worried about the poor chap's attack.'

Inspector Owen moved briskly to the door, and called. Sergeant Parry, tall, clean-shaven, young, came in. 'This is Dr. Griffiths. The specimen jar on the table is his. That's so isn't it, Doctor?' Inspector Owen's tone was suddenly official.

'Yes, it is.'

Inspector Owen turned to the police-sergeant. 'I want you to take possession of it. I am going to ring the Divisional Superintendent to see if it will be all right for you to take it to the police laboratory at Cardiff. Get the Super on the phone for me.'

Inspector Owen spoke on the telephone to the Superintendent of the division, Caernarvon, a case of suspected poisoning reported, and should he send Sergeant Parry to the laboratory at Cardiff with the specimen? Would that be all right?

All right by him, the Superintendent said and Inspector Owen hung up.

'Sergeant Parry will take it down to Cardiff,' he said to Dr. Griffiths.

'Meanwhile, what about Stone?'

'What about him?'

'I mean, giving him a warning?'

'You think it necessary?'

Dr. Griffiths gave a helpless shrug. 'I'm not used to coping with suspected murder every day. I think it would be wise for him to keep away from Merrill. Until we know the truth one way or the other.'

'I think I'd better keep quiet about it,' Inspector Owen said. 'If I looked in on him it might only arouse comment. You do it. You could drop a hint when you next see him. Tell him not to accept any more invitations from Merrill for the time being.'

Dr. Griffiths gave the other a nod and stood up slowly. 'Thanks,' he said. He smiled more cheerfully. 'I feel a bit of a load off my mind.'

'Not to worry,' the other said. 'It's probably a false alarm, and if it is, it's a secret between you and me. I'll let you know what I hear from Cardiff.'

Sergeant Parry took a train early that afternoon to Cardiff, the specimen-jar bulging his jacket pocket. It was a tedious journey with two changes. He reached the laboratory at five o'clock and handed the jar to Dr. Richards, with a request for the usual analysis to be made. 'Come back in an hour; I'll tell you what the reaction is,' Richards said.

Inspector Owen got the news on the telephone an hour later. Immediately after he had hung up on Sergeant Parry, he phoned Dr. Griffiths. 'You don't need to worry over your doubts about doing the right thing,' he said, 'if the information I've just received from Cardiff is correct.'

Next he phoned Caernarvon and spoke to the Superintendent, who in turn spoke to the Chief-Constable, named Pritchard. 'I'll get in touch with Scotland Yard,' Pritchard said. He put a call through to London, and a few minutes later he was speaking to the Assistant Commissioner, Crime.

2.

That same evening Philip Vane was chatting over a drink with a caller at his flat in Jermyn Street, and he was saying he had been up at Castlebay in North Wales. His caller said what a coincidence, because he happened to know that Superintendent Larrabee had left a couple of hours ago for Castlebay. Larrabee had taken Detective-Sergeant Pitt with him, and the murder bag.

Vane suddenly recalled Dr. Griffiths landing the

boss-trout, and muttering the name of Mrs. Merrill. Vane had seen Merrill a couple of days before in Castlebay. He had been with Dr. Griffiths who had told him that he had attended Merrill's wife, who had died a few months before. Why, Vane was now asking himself, had Dr. Griffiths been so interested in a patient who had died, so that it had taken his mind off the boss-trout? Doctors aren't usually all that anxious about a dead patient, they have enough thinking about their live ones.

Was Dr. Griffiths's sudden interest in Mrs. Merrill for a special reason, the same reason which had sent the two Scotland Yard detectives heading for North Wales? And whereas Dr. Griffiths might no longer be interested in the late Mrs. Merrill, Superintendent Larrabee might be very interested in her death, and what lay behind it.

After Vane's caller had gone he phoned a couple of people and then he drove through the night to arrive at Conway in the early hours. He had a feeling he would do better not to stay at Castlebay, instead he had fixed a room at the hotel at Conway.

He went down to breakfast at eight-thirty. As he went into the coffee room, there at a corner table sat Superintendent Larrabee and Detective-Sergeant Pitt.

CHAPTER FOUR

Superintendent Larrabee and Detective-Sergeant Pitt left the hotel at Conway in a police car Inspector Owen had sent, and a little while later they were in his office at Castlebay police station. Sergeant Pitt stood by the corner of the desk. Inspector Owen and Sergeant Parry sat facing the others.

'I have asked Dr. Griffiths and Mr. Stone to come in, in case you would like to see them,' Inspector Owen said. 'They are outside, now. Dr. Griffiths will probably want to get away.'

Dr. Griffiths came in and sat down in front of Superintendent Larrabee, as Inspector Owen introduced them.

'I see you attended the Merrills from about the time they first came to Castlebay,' the Scotland Yard man said, glancing up from the papers before him.

'I attended Mrs. Merrill. They came here about three years ago. Nothing ever seriously wrong with her, until she had her last illness. In January, six months ago.'

'And you also attended her husband, Mr. Merrill?'

'I think the first time would be about three or four months back. He was suffering from fibrositis, nothing serious. But, of course, I had got to know him well through my visits to his wife.'

'Mrs. Merrill was ill for how long?'

'She was ill for about a month.'

'You saw her husband during this last illness?'

Dr. Griffiths nodded. 'He was always inquiring how she was, and seemed very concerned that the illness was proving so obstinate to cure.'

'Did you find his attitude during her illness the least suspicious?'

'Naturally I didn't, otherwise I certainly should not have given the death certificate.'

Larrabee flashed him a bleak smile. Dr. Griffiths wondered if he was sounding pompous. 'It showed she died from Bright's Disease,' the detective said. 'You know anything about their private lives?'

'Nothing very much,' Dr. Griffiths smiled back. 'And if I did I shouldn't think it was my duty to tell you.'

'I understand. So far as you know they were living happily together?'

'So far as I know.'

'About how old was Mrs. Merrill?'

'She was thirty-seven when she died.'

'Her husband was younger, wasn't he?'

'Yes, he'd be about thirty-three.'

'It comes to this, then, Doctor. You felt no suspicion whatever about Mrs. Merrill's death until you attended Mr. Stone the other night. Is that right?'

'Yes; frankly, I don't quite know why, but I thought

he might be suffering from some form of poisoning, that's why I took a specimen. I told Inspector Owen here, I don't quite know what made me do that. Then while I was out the night before last, fishing, it suddenly flashed across my mind, this resemblance between his attack and Mrs. Merrill's illness. Perhaps it was just imagination, but I became uneasy about the whole matter. That was why I came to see Inspector Owen for advice. There may, of course, be no grounds whatever for my suspicions concerning Mrs. Merrill.'

Superintendent Larrabee was watching Inspector Owen filling his pipe. He let a little silence hang on the air before he turned back to Dr. Griffiths. 'Arsenic got into Mr. Stone's food,' he said, 'and it didn't get into his wife's, though they and Merrill ate the same meal. What's the fatal dose of arsenic?'

'I would say about two grains.'

'They found about seven-tenths of a grain in that specimen you took, which means that Stone must have had considerably more. We propose to see Merrill; you know, invite him to assist us in our inquiries. It may be, I wouldn't like to say at this stage, that we may have to go further than that. You understand, Dr. Griffiths? We may have to charge him with the attempted murder of Stone.'

'I fully understand the seriousness of what I've suggested about Merrill, if that's what you mean,' Dr. Griffiths said quietly.

'I am sure you do.'

Superintendent Larrabee didn't think it necessary to

add that if the situation was as dicey as that, he would have to decide about taking steps to obtain an exhumation of Mrs. Merrill.

'There still may be a very reasonable explanation for the arsenic getting into Mr. Stone's food,' Dr. Griffiths said, his face clouding over.

If there did turn out to be a reasonable explanation how arsenic got into Stone's food, Superintendent Larrabee thought, it would mean they might have to wait before asking for the exhumation. He realized Dr. Griffiths was speaking to him.

'I find it very hard to believe Merrill would poison his wife and attempt to poison a friend,' Dr. Griffiths was saying. 'I mean, for what motive?'

The other raised an eyebrow. Then his expression was bland and innocent. 'What indeed?' he said.

Dr. Griffiths found himself thinking about Dick Merrill and Mrs. Stone. His lips thinned and he gave a tiny sigh.

'Anyway,' the Scotland Yard man was saying, 'we're straying from purely medical considerations. You can leave motives to us. May I say that you did your duty by coming to Inspector Owen, and he will keep in touch with you.'

Dr. Griffiths went out and was quickly followed by a man of about fifty, tall and spectacled, with a moustache; he looked pale as though he had been through an exhausting illness. He appeared to be the unemotional type, and he just nodded to Superintendent Larrabee when Inspector Owen introduced them, indicating the chair Dr. Griffiths had sat in.

'I see you and your wife came to Castlebay about three years ago,' Superintendent Larrabee said.

Edward Stone nodded. 'I was employed in the Indian Civil Service, and I came home early in 1948. After India got her independence, that is. I met my wife about four years ago, and we decided to settle in Castlebay.'

'Your wife is younger than you?'

The eyes behind the horn-rims flickered over the detective. 'Considerably younger; she is only thirty.'

'And you have been living happily together?'

'We were very happy at first. Very happy, that is to say, until Merrill started his game.' The other eyed him questioningly. 'We met him and his wife at a party soon after we came to Castlebay. There wasn't anything definite until a few months ago, after Merrill lost his wife. Then I began to hear gossip that my wife had been seen with him in his car at one or two places; Llandudno, Conway was another. I spoke to Margot about it and she said he had just taken her for drives when I was away in London. That he was just a friend and nothing more.'

He broke off and took out a handkerchief and dabbed his forehead at the hairline, where spots of perspiration had formed. He folded the handkerchief carefully and put it back in his breastpocket so that only a little of it showed.

The others looked at him patiently. Edward Stone was not enjoying this very much.

'But the rumours that they had been seen about

together persisted,' he said, 'and I decided to confront him. I called at his office, and told him of the rumours I had heard. He appeared to take what I had said in the right spirit, and said he would not see my wife again.'

He paused once more, as if waiting for someone to say something.

'Go on, Mr. Stone,' Superintendent Larrabee said, 'was there any further trouble?'

'I discovered that he and my wife had again been meeting clandestinely. She admitted that she was attracted to him; she said he persuaded her to meet him and she could not resist. It was at this time that Merrill had invited my wife and me to dinner. We had accepted and were due to go to his house in a few days' time. I realized that I could not have a row with him at dinner, and had better see him immediately. I went along to his office.'

He brushed a finger and thumb along his moustache. 'Merrill admitted that he had met my wife again, but said the meeting was purely by accident. He may have flirted with her in a harmless way, but he assured me I should have no further ground for complaint. He sounded sincere, and so I saw no reason to doubt what he said. I told him we would still dine with him as arranged. He seemed very pleased at this, and then offered me some tea, but I refused. He pressed me to have it, but I still refused. I can't tell you why. Perhaps it is a good thing that I did.'

'And three nights ago, you went to Merrill's house with your wife for dinner?'

'I said I would go and I kept my word, and my wife went with me. It was a pleasant evening. Merrill was, of course, as charming as he well knows how to be. He is a woman's man, you know.'

'There was nothing out of the way about the dinner, nothing to attract your attention?'

'Nothing, but of course, I was not looking out for anything.'

Superintendent Larrabee glanced up from some notes on the desk. 'I see you had wine, and coffee afterwards. And still you saw nothing unusual or experienced nothing unusual?'

'When I began to talk about going, he said I must have a brandy for the road. At first I declined, and then I had some. Having had the brandy, my wife and I went shortly afterwards.'

'Did your wife not have any brandy?'

'No.'

Larrabee nodded as if to encourage the other to continue.

'I drove my wife home,' Stone went on. 'The journey was only about a couple of miles, and I felt nothing on the way. But soon after we got indoors I felt terribly ill in the stomach, and then I started to be sick. I was so ill all night that in the morning my wife decided to call Dr. Griffiths.'

'And he came to see you?'

'Yes.'

'And took a specimen?'

'I believe so, though I was too ill to note what he

was doing at the time.'

'Have you heard from Merrill since?'

'Yes, he phoned the next morning after the dinner party, and my wife told him I was ill. He phoned again next day, that was yesterday, and asked me to come and have tea at his office. I put him off. I told him I had been sick, and he said he couldn't understand it. Last night he phoned again to ask me to tea. By that time Inspector Owen had told me on no account should I accept any invitations from him. I again put him off.'

'So far as you know he kept away from your wife?'

'So far as I know.'

Superintendent Larrabee and Detective-Sergeant Pitt, accompanied by Inspector Owen, went to Dick Merrill's office in the High Street. Sergeant Parry drove them in a police car. They stopped outside the office, and Parry went in and told a clerk in the outer office that he had two visitors from London who would like to see Mr. Merrill.

Dick Merrill was smiling as Inspector Owen came in with the two plainclothes men and began to introduce them; Parry stood by the desk. Merrill stopped smiling when Inspector Owen said: 'Superintendent Larrabee and Detective-Sergeant Pitt are both from New Scotland Yard.'

'What in hell brings you to this part of the world?' Merrill's smile came back again as Sergeant Parry opened the door as if he'd heard someone outside, then he closed it and stood with his back to it.

'We have come to invite you to assist us in the

inquiries we are making about Mr. Stone's illness,' Superintendent Larrabee said. He made it sound reasonably conversational.

Merrill frowned. 'I know he's been sick, but he's all right again now; I spoke to him on the phone yesterday. Anyway, I should have thought Dr. Griffiths was the person you want. He's Stone's doctor and all that.'

'You see,' Superintendent Larrabee said, 'Mr. Stone was all right when he came to dinner at your house. But he was taken ill soon after he arrived home. I believe you were not taken ill?' He made it sound halfway between a statement of fact and a question.

'No, I was all right.'

'And his wife was not taken ill?'

'Mrs. Stone was all right; yes.'

'Can you explain why Mr. Stone alone should have been taken ill?'

Merrill shot him a look, his eyebrows drew together; his pale blue eyes glittered. 'What the devil is this? Why should I know any more than anyone else why he was ill?'

'You can't imagine why he should have been found to have been suffering from arsenical poisoning?'

'Arsenical poisoning? Good God, was that what it was? But look here, Inspector Owen,' and he turned to the uniformed figure. 'You're not suggesting I gave him arsenic, are you?'

'At the moment, sir,' Superintendent Larrabee said quietly, and Merrill's gaze came back to him, 'we're not suggesting anything. I'm merely trying to ascertain the facts. Would you care to make a statement?'

'I don't mind making a statement,' Merrill said briskly. 'But I don't see what the matter has got to do with me. What do you want to know?'

The detective didn't answer him. He sat there for a moment, pinching his thin nose with a bony finger and thumb. He spoke very softly. 'And then there's your late wife; we may have to make some inquiries about her.'

Merrill scowled at him incredulously. 'My late wife?'

'She died suddenly, didn't she?'

'Hardly, poor darling, she was ill some few weeks, but again I suggest you'd better ask Dr. Griffiths about that. He knows all about it.' He stared at them, his look searching their faces, one after the other; then he shrugged as if he had suddenly been transported to another plane of thought. 'But if you want a statement from me, about her or Stone, you can have it. I've nothing to hide.'

'You understand you are not obliged to say anything.' The other's tone was extremely warm and sympathetic. 'But anything you do say will be taken down in writing and may be given in evidence.'

'What does all that twaddle mean?' Merrill's voice was suddenly irritable.

'It's the usual caution to make quite clear that the statement you make is a purely voluntary one, and that it may be used in evidence if there should be any proceedings.'

'Any proceedings?'

'That's what I said.'

'All right,' Dick Merrill said, with a glance round as if humouring his visitors. 'I'm quite willing to make a statement.'

'To assist us in our inquiries?'

'If I can help you, I will.'

What he said was carefully written down by Sergeant Parry; and when the statement was completed Inspector Owen read it over to Merrill, who sat back listening.

'I have never had any arsenic in my possession,' his statement said. 'I have never had any need for it. I recall now that my wife may have had some arsenic for use in the garden. We had a fairly large garden at the back of our house, known as Fancy. I remember now the lawn at the back became infested with weeds, and my impression is that my wife purchased some arsenic to kill them.

'I think I may have suggested that she could get some arsenic from a local chemist for use in killing weeds. I'm almost sure it was Ivor Pryce. I think Ellen, my wife, always went to Pryce. She would be well-known there. So far as I know she used the arsenic for killing weeds.

'If any was left over it must have been thrown away, because I haven't seen any since. I certainly have not ever had any either at home or at my office. I think my wife got the arsenic two or three months before she died. She died last January.'

Dealing with her death, Inspector Owen read out

what Merrill had said: 'My wife and I lived fairly happily together. I married her nine years ago. She was five years older than I. She had been left quite a bit of money by her father, and quite frankly I suspected that people thought I married her simply for that. But although I was not deeply in love with her, I was very fond of her.

'Mrs. Stone and I were no more than friends. My wife was ill for about a month, and then she died. She had been getting very depressed at times, and I used to wonder whether she had taken anything to end her life. But she plainly hadn't, because I understood from Dr. Griffiths that she had died from Bright's Disease and acute gastritis.'

Dealing with Stone's illness: 'It is a complete mystery to me. If Mr. Stone suffered from arsenical poisoning, I've no idea where the poison came from. It certainly did not come from me. I have no motive whatever for seeking to put an end to his life.'

Merrill put his signature to each page of the statement, and Inspector Owen folded it and put the sheets of paper in his inside pocket. Superintendent Larrabee said the police would pursue their inquiries, and that if they needed any further information he had no doubt that Merrill would give them what assistance he could.

'Any time,' Merrill said.

Superintendent Larrabee said he would like to know who looked after Mrs. Merrill during her illness. Merrill said they had a housemaid named Gwladys Williams.

Sergeant Parry dropped the others back at the police station, and went over in the police car to interview Gwladys Williams in a nearby village, where she lived with her widowed mother. What she told him led him to ask her to come along to the police station and meet Inspector Owen and the men from Scotland Yard.

'I did not like the way Mr. Merrill was carrying on,' she said bluntly to Superintendent Larrabee. 'I never liked him very much. I'm sure he was already deceiving her with Mrs. Stone before his wife died. Anyway, you know Mrs. Stone used to come to Fancy after Mrs. Merrill died.'

Inspector Owen looked surprised. Gossip had not got hold of this titbit.

'I saw her there with him kissing one night. I heard him say: 'Why don't you leave him?' And Mrs. Stone said: 'I can't do that, Dick, much as I love you.' '

The conference at the Castlebay police station late that same afternoon reviewed the way things looked. And it did not look too simple to handle.

'He's a cool customer,' Superintendent Larrabee said, as he sat in Inspector Owen's office with the latter and Sergeant Pitt over a cup of tea. 'Got his wits about him. He knew perfectly well that his wife had bought arsenic and that we shouldn't have much difficulty in tracing it. So he slips in that she was buying it for killing weeds. You'll call on Pryce and all other chemists in the district, Serg.'

Sergeant Pitt nodded, while Larrabee turned to Inspector Owen. 'You remember he even went so far as to say that he may have suggested to his wife that she should buy arsenic for spraying and killing weeds. Very frank of him. Or could be he's relying on the fact that we've got no evidence that he was recently in possession of arsenic. Different kettle of fish if we had.'

Inspector Owen fiddled with his pipe glumly. 'We certainly can't charge him with attempted murder on the evidence as it stands,' he said. 'But if it turned out that his late wife and Stone suffered from the same kind of illness—'

'Only one died and the other didn't,' Superintendent Larrabee finished for him. 'But did Mrs. Merrill die from arsenical poisoning? That's the crux of this matter. Looks like there's nothing for it but to get Mrs. Merrill up.' He said it as if his mind had been made up some time. 'If you'd get me his nibs,' he said to Inspector Owen, 'I'll have a word with him.'

Inspector Owen had a call put through to the A.C.

CHAPTER FIVE

After Detective-Superintendent Larrabee and Detective-Sergeant Pitt had left the hotel for Castlebay, Philip Vane sat over his cup of coffee considering what his next move had better be.

He had got it out of Larrabee that he was interested in Mrs. Merrill's death six months before. He had also mentioned the illness of a certain Edward Stone. Obviously there was a link between the two. Larrabee wasn't so talkative; it was simply that he owed Vane a favour. In a way.

So, Larrabee would find out what he could from Dr. Griffiths and perhaps Stone; but it was unlikely he would leave the inquiries there.

A chat between him and Merrill was inevitable. Vane knew that Merrill had been the dead woman's husband. If a wife dies in suspicious circumstances, they usually start asking the husband questions. Sometimes he comes up with the answer they want. Though he and Pitt had taken the precaution of putting up at an hotel in Conway, strangers in Castlebay however discreet they acted, would be bound to attract notice. Sooner or later Merrill himself would get to know.

Larrabee would make himself known to Merrill as soon as he could. His idea would be to take him by surprise before gossip of the Scotland Yard detectives' arrival in Castlebay got around.

Of course, Merrill could satisfy Larrabee at once that any suspicions against him regarding his wife's death were completely unfounded. There were various ways by which he could prove his innocence, that there was nothing to it. For example, if he had been absent at significant times before or during his wife's death; or if he could prove that he had left all attendance upon her during that time entirely to a nurse and Dr. Griffiths.

Vane was working pretty much in the dark.

What had he got to go by? Dr. Griffiths's cryptic reference to Mrs. Merrill the night he'd caught the boss-trout, plus Scotland Yard's interest in her death and in someone named Edward Stone's recent illness. It was up to Vane to have something a bit more solid to go on.

The sort of information he needed could be picked up only by making inquiries on his own; and he wondered if perhaps he could think up some excuse to call upon Merrill himself. If all that he got out of him was that he had in fact been visited by the police, that at least would give Vane something. He would know for certain Merrill was under their suspicion. If so, then he should be able to decide by a bit more questioning, if Merrill had completely satisfied them.

Or if he had not.

Vane took a walk round Conway along down by the

quay and watched the fishing boats and the holiday-makers who had wandered down from the town, using the warm sunny day to take out rowing boats and dinghies.

He worked it out for himself that he might as well give Larrabee the chance to see Merrill before he dropped in on him, so it wasn't until after lunch that Vane drove over to Castlebay.

The office was a low-built, red-brick building on a corner. The clerk behind the mahogany-topped counter took his name and asked him to wait while he went into the office behind a half-glazed door. Vane heard voices and after a few moments the clerk came out and said that Mr. Merrill would see him. The clerk came from behind the counter and opened the half-glazed door again and announced him.

As the door closed behind Vane, Dick Merrill got up from behind the desk with a certain amount of puzzlement in his expression. 'What can I do for you?'

His office was old-fashioned, with dark-panelled walls and a long low window which looked out onto the back of the premises. It had obviously been smartened up but there was still a faintly old-fashioned atmosphere about it, despite the one or two examples of contemporary furniture. The usual framed certificates hung on the walls. On the desk, which was over-tidy, Vane noticed a large, silver-framed picture with its back towards him; he wondered if it was a photograph of Mrs. Merrill.

'The fact is,' Vane said, 'I expect to be engaged in

some business in this part of the world and I thought you may be able to help me.'

Merrill came round his desk with a steady stare from his pale eyes and indicated a leather-backed chair. Vane sat down while Merrill leaned against the mantelpiece above which was a mirror reflecting the back of his strong, tanned neck. He was wearing a nicely draped sports-coat and dark grey slacks meticulously creased above plain suede shoes. A spotted bow tie was tucked under his firmly moulded chin.

'What sort of business?'

'Let's say it's a little confidential at the moment,' Vane said.

'Let's say that, if you want,' Merrill said.

His reply wouldn't get the conversation much further, but Vane's object was to learn how cagey Merrill was. He supposed he might be able to decide whether for example Larrabee and Pitt had already been here before him or not.

Merrill's eyes had narrowed a little and he turned and picked up a paper-knife and tapped it against the edge of his desk.

'I don't want to give too much away,' Vane said, 'until I know how interested you would be the business.'

'Naturally I'm interested in most business.'

Vane got up from the chair and walked slowly over to the window and glanced out at the back walls of the houses opposite. He heard Merrill continue: 'For instance, what exactly *is* your business?'

'I'll put my cards on the table,' Vane said, still looking out of the window. It wasn't much of a view, but he knew the moment to turn and give him the old frank, man-to-man look. 'Other people's headaches are what I'm interested in.' This was where he turned on his heel slowly and gave him a little embarrassed grin. Merrill stared at him calculatingly.

Vane knew that Larrabee had been there before him.

'Go on,' Merrill said.

'I happen to be a lawyer, in a sort of way,' Vane said. 'I'm up here on holiday and I learned quite by chance that a couple of detectives have been making busybodies of themselves. It may very well be,' he went on, talking quickly, 'that they are wasting their time. But just in case they do make something of it, I'd like you to know I am on your side.'

'You say you're a lawyer and you've got some notion that the police are making inquiries about someone or something?'

Vane didn't tell him that he had been tipped off, naturally. He didn't say anything. Merrill did not appear curious. There was something about the set of his head on his neck that brought to Vane's mind's eye the image of the Jaguar at the side of the road caught in the lights of Dr. Griffiths's car and the two silhouettes close together. He knew then that one had been Merrill.

He thought he'd give the idea a whirl.

'That's quite a white Jag you have.'

Merrill never batted an eyelash. He smiled thinly.

'You're not fully informed,' he said. 'It isn't mine.'

A lot of things built up then fast inside Vane's skull. If the Jag wasn't his, chances were it was the woman's. And Dr. Griffiths had seen them together. That was what would have caused his delayed reaction thought about Mrs. Merrill. Seeing Merrill and another woman in the Jag like that. It fitted like the elusive piece in a jigsaw. Who had it been? Who was it Merrill was playing around with? Had he been playing around while his wife was alive? That was the next question that shaped up immediately after the first.

Vane tried another shot in the dark.

'And there's this business about Stone, you know.'

Merrill's thin smile looked as if someone had stuck it on.

Vane sat down in the leather-backed chair as casually as he could make it look. 'It's as simple as this,' he said. 'You may be in dead trouble and if you are you could need a little legal help.' Merrill didn't say anything and Vane went on. 'However trivial you may think this case is—'

'Case?'

'However cockeyed it may look from where you're sitting, I am sure you'll agree that a good lawyer never does any harm.'

There was silence for a few minutes while Merrill reflected about it. Vane took in the office a bit more. It seemed a little shabbier than it had been when he first came in; shadows seemed to have dusted the corners. Merrill stirred at his desk and he leant forward.

'What,' he said, 'do you want out of this?'

Vane put him in the picture, as much as he needed to be in it to keep him happy. At the end of it Vane gave him the bit about he might be wasting his time. 'The Scotland Yard dicks may be off back to the smoke this very minute, convinced they have got nothing to go on. I hope they have, for your sake.'

'I hope so, too,' Merrill said. 'All the same, I think you and I are in business.'

CHAPTER SIX

It was pushing three-thirty when Philip Vane left Merrill's office; and he called at the local newspaper and took a reporter named Davies for a cup of tea at a café. He was a grubby, shiny-eyed character and didn't sound too bright. But you couldn't have it both ways; if he'd been any brighter he would have started working out that there ought to be more in it for him. All Vane needed him to do was to keep his mouth shut and dig up all he could about Merrill, his late wife, and Stone.

As soon as Vane mentioned Stone, Davies stopped noisily swallowing his tea, and he fitted another piece into the jigsaw. Merrill and Mrs. Stone had been seen together, Davies said. Mrs. Stone was quite a piece. She was younger than her husband. Quite a bit younger.

When the British had pulled out of India, Edward Stone had arrived back in England a little while after his elder brother's death, and he had found himself with a sizeable private income on his hands. It had quite an impact; after having been unmarried all these years Stone had met a certain Margot Bell at a cocktail party and went overboard for her. Three months later this dullish, middle-aged man and this attractive young woman were married.

Stone took his wife on a motor-tour of North Wales for their honeymoon. They drove up the west coast from Barmouth to the Lleyn Peninsular. They drove from Harlech down to Pwllheli, back through Caernarvon and Conway, pausing at Castlebay.

It so happened that a bungalow-type house which a Liverpool business tycoon had built overlooking the estuary was up for sale. Stone saw it: it was called Tamarisk, and had an Eastern aura probably, reminiscent of Stone's life in India. There wasn't much his wife could do.

Then the Stones moved in and subsequently were introduced to the Merrills.

Vane impressed on Davies that he was to keep tabs on the Merrill situation, but not try anything on his own. Vane had started back to Conway when he made a sudden decision to call on Stone himself. He turned back to Castlebay, where he found the bungalow called Tamarisk. Just as he approached what he took to be the gates leading to the drive, a white Jaguar came out, and headed towards him. This was the car that Dr. Griffiths's Ford had outlined in the headlights, with two silhouettes inside, intimately close together. This could be Stone's wife, and then as the Jag flashed past Vane saw her face. It was her, for sure.

He drove past Tamarisk, reversed into the drive and chased after Mrs. Stone, making it fast in the direction he had come, and it occurred to him that she might be going into Conway to keep a rendezvous with Merrill.

He wondered if she had been delayed for some reason or other and was hurrying to get to wherever she was meeting Merrill on time.

Perhaps, Vane thought, his call at Merrill's office had delayed him, and then he wondered if on his way to the rendezvous Merrill might overtake the two of them. But the way she was taking the white Jaguar along it looked like Mrs. Stone was an habitually fast driver. She slowed through Conway and then turned up the hill to the hotel where Vane was staying and he guessed that this was the rendezvous.

Vane slowed up as she parked outside, and he watched her get out of the car. Her skirt was tight and her behind was small and rounded as she moved, fairly leisurely, into the hotel. Vane switched his thoughts and he noticed she hadn't taken the ignition key with her. Vane put his car into the garage; then he walked back, and he made it leisurely, to the hotel.

He was asking himself if she had any inkling of what had happened about Merrill, if she had learned that the Scotland Yard detectives had arrived in Castlebay, investigating not only her husband's illness but the death of Merrill's wife. It was unlikely, otherwise she surely would not be at the hotel waiting, which was Vane's guess, for Merrill.

But people in the sort of situation which she and Merrill had found themselves didn't react so normally. Hadn't they risked discovery that night, for instance, in the headlights of Dr. Griffiths's car? One thing about a secret love-affair was it produced a recklessness in the parties concerned. That way murder happened.

Vane was trying to think how to introduce himself to her. He had to do it before Merrill showed up, if he was due to show, or whoever else.

Then Vane passed the Jaguar and saw the ignition key.

He went into the hotel just in time to see the waiter at the corner table where she was alone and he overheard him say that she was wanted on the telephone. She got up and followed the waiter out of the lounge. Merrill, Vane thought, phoning to let her know he couldn't make it, or he would be late.

She was away several minutes, and when she came back Vane was watching her face, and it did not seem to have changed. It gave him no indication that she was upset or annoyed, or scared or angry. The waiter was at her table and she was ordering tea. Vane hesitated a few moments then he started towards her.

'You left this in your car,' he said.

She looked up at him casually, and then saw the ignition key and the St. Christopher tag. The tag was enamel and silver, and on the back was inscribed: 'Take care of darling Margot.' She gave him the impression this was something she was always forgetting to remember, to take the ignition key with her.

She glanced at her watch. 'I ought to be going,' she said.

Vane looked at her steadily.

'What's the rush?' he said. 'Why don't you stay and have a drink? If you don't have to hurry back to your husband, stay a little longer, at any rate and have a drink with me.'

'I would like that,' she said. 'I would very much like a gin-and-soda.'

Vane made it scotch-and-soda for himself.

The ignition key introduction had worked. He had chatted about the Jag, and then he lit a cigarette for her; and then he was sitting at her table, and she was asking him about his car, and he had talked to her about that, how it was a souped-up job and that he had managed to come up to North Wales from London averaging 40 m.p.h. And the other cars he had driven, down Le Route Bleu and the autobahns.

'It's the sort of thing I'd like to have gone in for,' she had said. 'Driving cars; most of my boyfriends drove them fast, and I still get a kick out of putting my foot down. This part of the world the roads aren't quite up to the roads you've mentioned.'

By now, people had come in from their boating or fishing and the shadows were beginning to obtrude from outside, while the Welsh waiter got another gin for her, and scotch for him.

'I'd love to see your car,' she said, and he gave her a smile over his drink and they got up from the table and went out of the hotel. She slipped her arm through his as they turned round the corner of the hotel down to the garage.

He lifted the bonnet of the car and described the inside to her. He played the radio a little and explained the gadgets to her, the heating-device and the rev counter he had fitted below the dash.

'Why not let me take you for a spin?' he said.

'I'm not fussy,' she said and began to get into the car as he held the door open for her.

He got into the driving seat and then turned to her and said: 'I always like to have an objective when I'm driving. Let's go somewhere for eats.'

'Okay,' she said.

'Be okay with your husband?'

'He's not expecting me back until later on.'

She let a little smile play around the corners of her mouth. He had a sudden feeling she knew what his game was.

Only he didn't see how she could know.

CHAPTER SEVEN

Over coffee she asked him was he married himself. Vane didn't make a production of it; he played it modest and said the right girls he had met didn't think he was the right man. Anyway, it gave her the lead in to what she wanted to tell him.

They were in the dining room of the little pub in Beddgelert. There was another couple at the end of the dark-beamed room, but the waiter had put Vane and Margot Stone at a table with a view of the hump-bridge over the river.

She had come up with a certain amount about how she'd been in the fashion model racket before she'd married Stone; how she'd looked forward to a good time in London, jaunts to Italy and the South of France. But as it had turned out Castlebay wasn't too rugged. Sailing on the estuary, driving the Jag her husband had given her for a wedding present. Several trips to London.

Then she had led into the chat about marriage; now she began about a married woman friend who had been discussing with her, Margot Stone said to Vane, having an affair with someone she'd met.

Margot Stone was talking about herself. She was much more relaxed now. She grew serious as she asked him what he thought of the idea of a married woman having a love affair with another man. She was smoking nervously and quickly.

He thought, he said, it depended on circumstances.

'Supposing the wife was sure it can't hurt the husband; that he will never know?'

'You ever known,' he said, 'where the husband never knew that his wife was having an affair with somebody else?'

'Do you really mean that?' she said. 'So you really believe it's impossible for a husband not to know if his wife's in love with someone else?'

'Not impossible,' he said, 'only damned unlikely.'

She fell silent and took a deep, deep drag at her cigarette.

He watched her exhale slowly and thoughtfully, and a feeling of pity for her stirred within him. Not much pity, but he felt sorry for her after a fashion.

'It can depend,' he said, 'a great deal on the man whether it's a good idea that somebody else's wife should fall in love with him, and he with her.'

'I don't think he can help himself very much,' she said. 'He's a widower. His wife died several months ago.'

'Was he in love with his wife?'

'I don't think so,' she said. 'I don't see how he could have been.'

'What makes you think that?'

'For a start she wasn't all that attractive and secondly she had the money.'

'So your friend,' he said, 'she's wasting her time anyway. I am never one to pass any moral judgments, but she can't really think much of a chap who marries a woman simply for what he can get out of her.'

'You are being a stuffed shirt,' she said. 'Many a marriage has worked out between two people who didn't love each other in that way, but simply saw each other as a good financial proposition.'

The way she was talking Vane came to the conclusion then that she didn't suspect anything. She had not even been smart enough to mask the identity of the two people she was talking about; she must have given herself away if she had any idea Merrill's wife had been murdered, if she had been. She would be equally ignorant of Merrill's attempt, if he had made any, on her husband's life.

She switched the topic; Vane got the bill and they went out into the bar, and they each had a brandy, and then they went out of the pub. Now it was quite dark and bats were overhead, dipping and twisting against the trees. It was under the shadow of a tree that Vane stopped. Below the still, snow-capped mountain peaks the woods were black. As she turned to him, her eyes questioning in the shadow, he bent and kissed her. She made it into a long kiss.

They went back to the car and got in and he switched the sidelights on, so that the green light of the dash gave her face a faintly ghostly glow. They drove off back the way they had come. In the headlights the road twisted and curved away before them, and she turned on the radio. Presently the sad tune of *La Vie en Rose* trailed on the night.

He stopped the car.

He knew for certain it was Merrill she had been going to meet. She wasn't wearing a bra; or anything under her skirt.

It was about two hours later when they arrived back at the hotel at Conway and he put his car into the garage. His arm around her waist, they walked back in the gathering darkness to the Jaguar, a ghostly gleam outside the hotel. She got in without a word and gave him a long look in the light reflected from her headlights.

'Ships that pass in the night,' she said.

'I'll keep a look out for you,' he said.

He stood watching the taillights disappear down the street; then he walked slowly back to the garage and got the car round to the front of the hotel. There was no sign of Larrabee or Pitt when he went in. He looked at his wristwatch. It had turned eleven o'clock; the boys were working late. He went upstairs and packed, he paid his bill, took his suitcase out to the car, and drove over to Castlebay.

He thought he might have a chat with Davies before he pushed off back to London.

His headlights picked out some figures ahead and he saw there were two cars at the side of the road. He was approaching the Castlebay church and he slowed. He braked and watched. He knew what was going on all right, and he didn't have to get out of the car to find out any more about it.

He didn't need to talk to Davies; there was nothing for him except turn back for London.

CHAPTER EIGHT

1.

The police car had met Dr. Henry Mortlake at Conway off the Holyhead train, at 10:14 that night. The Assistant Commissioner had moved quickly after Superintendent Larrabee's phone call in the afternoon and Dr. Mortlake had caught the 5:25 p.m. from London.

He went straight to the churchyard; with him were Chief-Constable Pritchard, Superintendent Larrabee, Inspector Owen, Detective-Sergeant Pitt and the rest of them. The cemetery superintendent and the grave-digger; the undertaker Morgan the Coffin; there was the pathologist and a chemist from Cardiff police laboratory. It was thought right that Merrill himself should know what was in the wind, and he was informed of the exhumation, and so was Dr. Griffiths.

Merrill, on being told Dr. Griffiths would be there, stayed away.

Behind canvas screens the grave was opened up in the light of oil lamps. First, samples were taken from the soil in various parts of the cemetery, to ascertain whether there was arsenic in the soil. They were placed in various containers and sealed.

Mrs. Merrill's grave was identified by the cemetery superintendent and the gravedigger. Digging then began, and a sample of the soil was collected from immediately above the coffin, Morgan duly identifying it. Further samples of soil were taken, and the coffin was raised by Morgan and the gravedigger, who trundled it on a hand-bier to a semi-derelict cottage in the lane by the churchyard.

Sacking was hung over the front room window, and by the light of more oil lamps, Dr. Mortlake made his preliminary examination.

The remains were reinterred, and Dr. Mortlake made a dash in the police car to catch the Holyhead train back to London, which was stopped for him at Conway at 1:28 a.m. In the sleeper with him were the specimens in jars for analysis. It had been quite a busy night for him and he slept well.

A Scotland Yard car met him off the train at Euston at 6:45 a.m. That afternoon the Home Office analyst, Kilrain, reported to him what the specimens from the grave at Castlebay showed.

At 4:25 p.m. Superintendent Larrabee, accompanied by Sergeant Pitt and Inspector Owen, made a second call upon Merrill. He was just leaving his office to go home. But he didn't go home. Not that evening.

'You know who I am,' Larrabee said, without wasting much time discussing the weather. 'As a result of the exhumation of the body of your late wife it has been ascertained that she died from arsenical poisoning.'

Merrill stared at him, wooden-faced. Larrabee took

a deep breath and went on. 'I am therefore going to arrest you and take you to Castlebay police station, and there you will be charged with the wilful murder of your late wife; and you will also be charged with the attempted murder of Edward Stone. It is right that I should tell you that you are not obliged to say anything unless you wish to, but anything you say will be taken down in writing and may be given in evidence.'

'I shall deny that I had anything to do with the death of my wife or the illness of Mr. Stone,' Dick Merrill said. 'Perhaps you would let me telephone my solicitor. He is in London.'

2.

Royston, who was a partner in the firm of police-court solicitors which Philip Vane had once had a part of before he went inside, caught the 5:25 p.m. for Conway, and was able to see Merrill late that night at Castlebay police station.

Next day he was brought before Castlebay Magistrate's Court. Afterwards, Royston phoned Vane in London and filled in the picture. He had talked to Morgan the Coffin, the people at the cemetery, Sergeant Parry at the police station, Gwladys Williams and others. He was in court when Inspector Owen went into the witness box formally to prove the arrest of the accused.

Inspector Owen said the matter was in the hands of the Director of Public Prosecutions, and he asked for a remand of eight days, when he said the prosecution hoped to be in a position to proceed. Royston had no objection to offer, Dick Merrill was duly remanded, and taken in a police car to Caernarvon Jail.

Royston saw him in the afternoon and got from him a detailed statement concerning his life with his late wife, his acquaintanceship with Edward Stone, and his interviews with the police, the statement he had made to Superintendent Larrabee of which Royston would obtain a copy in time for the next police court hearing.

Vane heard it in full from Royston on his return to London. He had been wondering how Margot Stone had taken it; he hadn't told Royston about her. He killed an impulse to go up to Castlebay, to try and see her again. It was an impulse, he decided, which was best left where it was; he didn't think it would get him anywhere.

But he couldn't help wondering how she and Stone were getting on; and how sick she felt for Merrill's sake.

3.

At the next hearing eight days later, before the same magistrate, Claud Smithson from the Director of Public Prosecutions Office told the court that, according to the prosecution, arsenic had been administered by the accused to Stone, and that this had led to the exhumation of the body of the accused's wife, with the result that her remains were also found to contain the same poison.

It was not necessary, Smithson said, for the prosecution to say what the motive was, but he thought it right to mention that the case for the prosecution was that the accused was actuated by a passionate devotion to Mrs. Stone and his desire to get rid of those who stood in the way of his fulfilment of it, his wife and Edward Stone.

'That's a lie,' Merrill said from the dock, his voice raised angrily. He showed increasing agitation as Claud Smithson unfolded the case for the prosecution.

'Tell your client he must not interrupt the proceedings,' the magistrate's clerk told Royston. 'The court will hear anything he has to say in due course.'

Then the business of taking the witnesses' depositions: Gwladys Williams, enjoying the opportunity it gave her of telling the story of Dick Merrill's carrying on with Mrs. Stone; Dr. Griffiths frankly admitting that he had been misled by appearances; Dr. Richards, Cardiff police laboratory analyst; and Dr. Mortlake; there was Edward Stone to add his account of the dinner party at Tamarisk, and its consequences.

Royston made no attempt at any cross-examination; he was careful not to risk tying counsel's hands at the trial, if a trial should follow. 'No questions,' he said at the end of each of the witnesses' evidence.

And then Mrs. Stone entered the witness box; as she took off her glove to hold the Testament, she looked across at Dick Merrill and smiled; it was a fleeting smile and he smiled back at her.

She was clearly essential to the prosecution as a witness. She could describe what had transpired that night at the dinner party and of her husband's illness. But Claud Smithson catching that smile exchanged between her and Merrill interpreted it as an indication of what might be ahead.

She gave her evidence hesitantly, her voice was quiet, but she could be heard quite clearly. She gave an account of what had happened at the dinner party. Smithson did not ask her any questions about her friendship with Merrill; he left it to the defence.

Royston knew he was on safe ground, and this time when Smithson had finished, he stood up. 'Mrs. Stone, you saw nothing unusual at the dinner party?'

'Nothing whatever.'

'You did not see the accused act in a suspicious manner?'

'Certainly not. He was charming to us both, as he always was.' And again she smiled at Merrill. This time he did not smile back at her, but gave her a little nod.

'No more charming to you than to your husband?'

She looked at Royston, her face serious, and then said: 'No, I think not.'

'Did you know his maidservant, Gwladys Williams?'

'I really could not say whether I did or not.'

Royston's glance flickered from her to Merrill, then he asked for Gwladys Williams to stand up in court. She came and stood by the witness box. Margot Stone said: 'No, I don't think I have ever seen her before.'

'Does that mean that you have never been to the bungalow known as Fancy, alone?'

'I have been to Fancy once or twice by myself, but I can't remember the exact occasions.'

And there Royston left it; all the prosecution's evidence had been offered and Royston submitted that there was no *prima facie* case.

'No reasonably-minded jury,' he said, 'could convict the prisoner of murder on the evidence as it stood. The only case against him was that Mrs. Merrill died from the effects of arsenic, which may have been self-administered or administered by accident. And that Mr. Stone, also in some mysterious way, suffered from the effects of arsenical poisoning.'

There was no evidence to show, he went on, that his client even had arsenic in his possession, and certainly there was no evidence that he ever used it in the way alleged.

Merrill watched the magistrates, one woman and two men, intently as they went out to their retiring room. They were back in ten minutes, to whisper with the clerk, who nodded affirmatively before turning to look at Royston.

'We find on the evidence as it stands that there is a *prima facie* case.'

There was a mutter in the court, which was full, and the clerk coughed loudly before he turned to Merrill, glancing down at the note in his hand.

'You will have an opportunity to give evidence on oath before us, and to call witnesses. But first I am going to ask you whether you wish to say anything in answer to the charges? You need not say anything unless you wish to do so; and you have nothing to hope from any promise, and nothing to fear from any threat, that may have been held out to induce you to make any admission or confession of guilt. Anything you say will be taken down and may be given in evidence at your trial. Do you wish to say anything in answer to the charges?'

Royston was up on his feet again. 'Through me, sir, the accused pleads Not Guilty to both charges, and reserves his defence.'

The clerk gave him a nod, coughed again and then committed Dick Merrill to stand his trial at the next Assizes, mid-October at Caernarvon.

CHAPTER NINE

1.

One evening, about a week before the expected date when the trial was set to open, there was a consultation with leading counsel for the Crown. The Attorney-General, Sir Bertram Ainger, Q.C., had been briefed by the Director of Public Prosecutions, and his junior was Francis Wells. Sir Bertram's clerk was opening the door of his principal's room at the Courts of Justice. Ainger was at his desk covered with papers; he looked up over his pince-nez.

'Are you ready, Sir Bertram? Mr. Wells is here and Mr. Smithson, from the Director's Office.'

Wells was a burly figure, and he followed Smithson into the room. 'This is an interesting case, I must say,' Ainger said, as the others sat down. 'No developments since the committal, I suppose?'

'Nothing beyond the depositions,' Smithson said. 'No additional evidence.'

'I understand Harry Deveen is to appear for the defence.' Ainger pushed the papers aside and leant against the corner of his desk. 'I shall be very surprised if he does not object to the admissibility of the evidence relating to Stone.' He had a soft, musical voice in conversation, which became harsher in court. 'He will say, I suppose, that the case relating to Mrs. Merrill can't possibly be affected by what happened months afterwards in the case of somebody else, the man Stone. I must say, that it is a bit extraordinary.'

'You have looked at the Armstrong Case?' Wells said.

Ainger nodded. 'It's thirty-five years ago, but it's none the worse for that. It supports the view that Stone's case is admissible as throwing light on the earlier case of Mrs. Merrill, as evidence of design. That is, of course, assuming that Merrill had access to arsenic before the death of his wife and at the time of the Stone business.'

Wells and Smithson exchanged glances; the danger, they knew lay in trying to pin it on Merrill if they had to rely solely on the evidence concerning his wife's death.

'If he had access to it,' Ainger was saying, 'the fact that he was using arsenic for a deadly purpose in the case of Stone is evidence from which the jury might infer that he had it for no innocent purpose during the illness of his wife.' He paused, moved away from the desk, his hands deep in his pockets. 'But where is there any evidence of his possession of arsenic?'

'Surely what he said in his statement may be very significant?' Wells said. 'You will remember he said that he may have suggested to his wife that she purchase some arsenic for killing weeds.'

'That's in his statement,' Smithson said. Ainger pursed his mouth up judiciously, while Smithson went on. 'The jury may think that he was merely using his wife as a means of achieving his own ends, and he would think it prudent to keep his name off the poisons register.'

'All the same,' Ainger said, 'there is nothing to negate his statement that his wife used the arsenic for killing weeds, and that any that was left over must have been thrown away.'

'Only,' Wells said, 'that both Mrs. Merrill and Stone suffered from arsenical poisoning. If the jury think that Mrs. Merrill did not commit suicide, may that not be enough?'

Ainger took off his pince-nez and replaced them on his nose. 'The case against Merrill will be all that weaker if Deveen can succeed in shutting out the evidence about Stone,' he said with an air of finality. 'And I do not think he will succeed in doing that. It seems to me the position is very similar to the Armstrong Case—'

'To which this bears certain resemblances,' Smithson said.

'I should have thought the only resemblance was that here, too, you have Merrill suspected of poisoning his wife, who died, and a man who didn't.'

Wells's tone was a little impatient. He wanted to keep to the point, which was this Merrill business, and not hark back to an old murder case which to him possessed only superficially relevant features.

'That is what Armstrong did,' Ainger said. 'Poisoned

his wife with arsenic and tried to poison his friend.'

'But this friend wasn't the husband of a woman Armstrong was in love with,' Wells said.

Ainger sat on the corner of the desk again. 'The point is,' he said patiently, 'that in the Armstrong business it was ruled that this other evidence was admissible for the purpose of proving that the deceased wife actually died of arsenic; that her death was not accidental; and that it was not inadmissible by reason of its tendency to prove or create a suspicion of a subsequent felony. From the defence point of view the damage has already been done; the jury will know all about Stone's poisoning. In fact, I think that all this publicity about the case coming up for trial may prove awkward for the defence. I think newspapers should be silenced until the actual trial takes place.'

Wells made an impatient movement again. Now Ainger was going to climb on to his pet hobby-horse; but Ainger took off his pince-nez, looked at it, replaced it and said: 'However, that is merely my own opinion. I am sure Deveen will see that his client has a good run.' He paused and eyed the others. 'Well that's all,' he said. 'Unless there's anything either of you would like to discuss?'

'I don't think there's anything,' Wells said.

'Nothing I want to raise,' Smithson said. 'Mr. Justice Lane is the judge,' he added.

'He's a good judge,' Ainger said, 'but I do not think he'll agree to let Deveen shut out the evidence about Stone. However, we shall see.'

2.

The morning following the consultation in Ainger's room at the Courts of Justice, Royston had arranged for Harry Deveen to accompany him to Caernarvon Jail, where they were to have a conference with Dick Merrill.

Royston rapped the knocker on the small door at the side of the main gates of the prison. There was silence for a few moments before heavy footsteps were heard inside. A prison officer opened the door, and they followed him into a large room on the right, where they signed the visitors' book. Another prison officer appeared and took them to the room where they were to interview Dick Merrill.

They went along a broad passage, passing a prisoner wearing a grey prison uniform, then came to a room reserved for prisoners. They went in and sat together on one side of the large table. They didn't chat to each other while they waited.

A minute or so later another prison officer appeared in the doorway with Dick Merrill, who sat down. The officer stepped just outside, where he remained during the interview, glancing in from time to time through the glass panels of the door.

Merrill looked to be in good health, and appeared relaxed.

Royston introduced him, saying, 'This is Mr. Deveen, who is appearing for you at the trial.'

Deveen shook hands with him. 'I have to make sure that I know all you can tell me about your case. I have, of course, read the statement which you made to the police, and all the instructions which your solicitor has carefully prepared. Is there anything else I ought to know?'

Merrill looked at him with interest. Harry Deveen wore a dark suit, neatly cut and a dark, knitted tie. He was of medium height with an ageless look about his sharp-featured face.

'I don't think there is,' Merrill said. 'Though I wouldn't mind if you'd let me know what you think of my chances.' He was smiling a little.

Deveen replied with a thinnish sympathetic smile. 'Frankly,' he said, 'I shall be in a much better position to tell you when I know whether the evidence about Stone is to be admitted or not. By itself the evidence about your wife is all very vague. The jury may think it possible the arsenic was self-administered or that she took it by accident. But the case may look very different once they have the evidence about Stone.'

'But haven't they got to show that I was in possession of arsenic?'

Harry Deveen glanced at him. Merrill was evidently fully aware of the essence of the case which the prosecution would seek to make against him.

'No doubt,' Deveen said, 'the jury have got to be satisfied about that before they can convict you.'

Merrill leaned back in his chair, eyed Royston for a moment, then looked hard at Deveen. 'I don't see how they can be satisfied about that. I knew perfectly well the police would find out that my wife had purchased arsenic. That's why I told them all about it. But they can't trace any arsenic to me. As I said I never had any either at home or at my office, and that's the truth. Is there anything else you want to know?'

'About your wife. The jury will want to know what you thought of her?'

'I mentioned this in my statement, didn't I?'

'You will have to speak the truth if you are asked about it.'

'What do you mean, if I am asked about it?'

'I mean that you may be asked about it when you are in the witness box. You will have to answer as truthfully as you can the questions which are put to you. Don't underestimate the jury. The jury can very quickly size up a witness who is shifty or not truthful. If you are perfectly honest about your wife it may well help you on other issues in the case.'

'I was absolutely straightforward about her to the police,' Merrill said. 'I told them frankly that I married her because I was fond of her, as well as because of her money. I admitted then that I never loved her, and I'll say the same in the witness box. That's what you want me to say, isn't that what you mean?'

'I think we understand each other perfectly,' Harry Deveen said.

'But because I didn't love her doesn't mean that I murdered her,' Merrill persisted. 'Why should I? What motive? For her money? I was doing all right as it was; the money she left me in her will is going to be taken up by death duties and the rest of it, so I'm really worse off by her death.'

'I don't think the question of motive need enter into it,' Deveen said quietly. 'The prosecution won't suggest any.'

'I see,' Merrill said. 'I thought it might be important.'

'You're going to be all right; try not to worry.'

'I'll leave all that to you, eh?'

'Mr. Royston will be in close touch with you during the trial, and if there is anything you want me to know, contact him.'

Merrill stood up, and the prison officer came in. Harry Deveen shook hands with him. After he had muttered some words of thanks, Merrill went out with the prison officer.

CHAPTER TEN

Early in the morning, Monday, 15th October, 1956, the queue had started outside the old red building at Caernarvon where the Assizes were held. Punctually at ten-thirty Mr. Justice Lane's entry into the court-room was heralded by three sharp knocks on the door.

Bewigged and wearing scarlet robes trimmed with ermine, his small stature was suitably exaggerated, so that he looked considerably taller than he was. He was in his sixties, and was thin-faced, with a long straight nose. He was carrying white gloves and the black cap. With him was his clerk, a middle-aged man in morning coat, who sat next to him in the high-backed chair.

When Detective-Superintendent Larrabee and Philip Vane saw each other during the trial, Vane mentioned what a small world it was that it should be the same judge he had been up before, at the Old Bailey. It was Larrabee who had arrested Vane. Which is why he sort of owed him a favour. Vane had kept his mouth shut at the time; he could have opened wide about how someone else involved had been allowed to slip quietly away to South America.

But then Vane's motto was: 'Always keep in with

the law.'

Just as the judge bowed to the Court and the Court bowed back in return, Dick Merrill came up the steps from the cells into the dock.

He looked confident and composed, no sign of strain or apprehension. That might come later, especially in the witness box; and Harry Deveen was putting him in the box for sure. With him were two blue-uniformed prison officers. Merrill bowed to the judge, and then sat down on a plain wooden chair near the front of the dock.

The Clerk of Assize sitting below the judge stood up and looked at Merrill, who got to his feet. Reading from the indictment he told him that he was charged with the wilful murder of his wife, Ellen Merrill, at Castlebay.

'How say you, are you Guilty or Not Guilty?'

'Not Guilty.'

The Clerk of Assize then called the jurors into the jury box. They clumped in a trifle self-consciously, nine men and three women. 'Members of the Jury in waiting, please answer to your names and step into the jury box as you are called.'

It was routine stuff.

One after another of the nine men and three women took their places in the jury box, looking like any jury trying hard to use their common sense; they were all local people. Each had to stand up to be sworn in; and then the black-gowned usher stood in the well of the courtroom and did his piece about asking anyone to come forward if they knew anything about the prisoner that the court ought to know.

A brief silence before the Clerk of the Assize turned to tell the jury the substance of the charge against Dick Merrill; and then Ainger got to his feet to open the case to the jury, taking off his pince-nez and then clipping them back on his high-bridged nose. Behind him sat Wells. To his left sat Harry Deveen and Gordon Snell, Deveen's junior; at a table in front of counsel, Smithson and Royston.

'May it please you, my lord, members of the jury,' Ainger began, but before he got any further, Harry Deveen was up on his feet, his shark-like face pushed forward underneath his wig.

'My lord, there is a submission I would like to make,' he said, 'before my friend opens this case.'

It was foreseeable stuff, and the judge said: 'Presumably you don't wish the jury to remain?'

Deveen said he didn't want the jury in and there was a clatter as they filed out to their retiring room. Deveen glanced at the Attorney-General who was looking up at the judge.

'I do not know,' Deveen said, 'what course my learned friend intends to take, but I should like your lordship to know at the earliest possible moment that on the charge of murder I shall object to the admissibility of any evidence in the Stone case. It is inadmissible on this charge as read from the depositions.'

Mr. Justice Lane nodded, and he squinted down his nose at Ainger who got on his feet. 'On this indictment,' he said to Ainger, 'are you calling the evidence relating to the alleged poisoning of Stone?'

Ainger said he proposed to do so, and the judge turned to Deveen.

'My lord,' Deveen said, 'my submission is that the evidence relating to the Stone case is of no relevance whatsoever to the charge your lordship has here of murder.' He gave a little deprecatory cough. It was a trick of his when speaking to the judge, as if to say he regretted having to remind him of something that was, of course, obvious to his superior intelligence.

'As your lordship knows,' Deveen said, 'the general rule is that evidence on a criminal charge is to be confined to the facts of the particular case which the jury is trying. No doubt my friend will submit that there are exceptions, and will endeavour to show that the case on which the prisoner is charged was due to design and not accident. But the prisoner denies that he poisoned his wife, and so it is left to the Crown to establish their case beyond reasonable doubt. Surely it is not open to the Crown to attempt to prove that the prisoner poisoned his wife by calling evidence to show that months afterwards he attempted to poison someone else, which attempt he also denies?'

'Is there any doubt,' the judge said, 'that Mrs. Merrill died from arsenical poisoning?'

'My lord, I can make no admission as to that, it is for the Crown to prove their case. There certainly is evidence that Mrs. Merrill died from arsenical poisoning.'

'Then will not the jury have to answer whether Mrs. Merrill died from arsenical poisoning, and if she did, whether it was designed by somebody else, or whether it was suicide or accident?'

Harry Deveen said that the one issue for the jury would be whether the evidence established beyond reasonable doubt that Merrill had poisoned his wife. That issue ought not to be confused by a suspicion that Merrill may have attempted long after to poison somebody else. The two cases should be kept distinct.

Deveen referred to the Armstrong Case; Geering's Case, a subsequent Australian case decided in the Privy Council; a baby-farming case, where a husband and wife accused of murdering an infant whose body was found buried in the garden of their house, and evidence of infants' bodies having been found buried in the gardens of several houses previously occupied by them was held to be relevant; another case decided by the Privy Council where the conviction of a man charged with murdering a woman by potassium cyanide poisoning was quashed; and another case where the House of Lords had considered a series of eight thefts having common characteristics.

Deveen wasn't leaving it to Ainger to cite any case against him.

It was Ainger's turn. 'The evidence,' he said, 'relating to the Stone case is, in my submission, admissible on this charge, my lord. I shall ask the jury to infer from all the evidence which I shall place before them that the prisoner was in fact in possession of arsenic, and that will be a matter for the jury in considering the evidence in the Stone case. It will surely help the jury to decide whether Mrs. Merrill's death was designed by the prisoner or whether it was suicide, or whether it was the result of an accident.'

He sat down. There was a brief pause, then the judge went ahead and based his decision on the Armstrong Case. In his view it completely covered the present case.

'The Crown,' he said, 'are entitled to use the evidence relating to Stone for the purpose of showing, if they can, that Mrs. Merrill actually died of arsenical poisoning; that her death was not accidental. In my opinion, for the reasons I have briefly given, the evidence in the Stone case is admissible and I rule accordingly.'

Harry Deveen hitched his gown about his shoulders in a sort of shrug. It was a decision of vital importance; it made the case against Merrill more formidable. But if the judge had made a mistake, if it was wrong in law, and Merrill was convicted, it meant that the conviction could be set aside by the Court of Criminal Appeal. So it had its bright side, in a way.

But he did not look at Dick Merrill in the dock.

The jury were back into their places and Ainger was dealing with Mrs. Merrill's illness.

'Members of the jury, at the time of her death Dr. Griffiths thought the symptoms were due to natural causes, but late in July, the attention of the Director of Public Prosecutions was drawn to the case, and Home Office experts were consulted.

'Mrs. Merrill's remains were duly exhumed, and Dr. Mortlake found on analysis that in the curiously well-preserved remains, and in the organs which alone he dealt with, there were nearly three-and-a-half grains of arsenic. More than a fatal dose was therefore discovered in parts of the body several months after death; death which was undoubtedly due to arsenical poisoning to which Mrs. Merrill had been subjected during the last weeks of her life. A final dose had been administered within twenty-four hours of her death. You will have no doubt that she died, not from any natural causes, but from arsenical poisoning.'

The jury, he told them, might have to consider three possibilities. Did Mrs. Merrill take arsenic accidentally? Did she commit suicide? Or was she murdered? The case for the Crown was that she was murdered, and murdered by her husband, Richard Merrill.

Mrs. Merrill was a few years older than her husband, Ainger went on, and the jury might come to the conclusion that he had tired of her. Not only that, they might well think that he had formed an attachment for another man's wife, for Mrs. Stone; and the case for the Crown was that Merrill wanted his wife out of the way, and that he also wanted Mrs. Stone's husband out of the way, and that he employed the same means to achieve these two ends: arsenic.

'An important witness in this case is Dr. Griffiths,' Ainger said. 'Of course, it never entered his mind that her husband was slowly killing Mrs. Merrill, so that when she eventually died, Dr. Griffiths certified that her death was due to Bright's Disease and gastritis. It was only when he had to attend Stone that it occurred to him that Stone's symptoms were the same as those from which Mrs. Merrill was suffering before she died.'

It was Dr. Griffiths's suspicion which had started the investigations, as a result of which a remarkable coincidence, Ainger said, had emerged. The coincidence that Mrs. Merrill had died from arsenical poisoning. And Stone very nearly did so.

'The evidence relating to Stone's illness,' Ainger said, 'will assist you in deciding whether Mrs. Merrill's death was designed by the prisoner, and if he attempted to poison Stone. If that is proved, then it will help you to decide that he also poisoned his wife. The Crown is not in the position to call into evidence that the prisoner was in actual possession of arsenic at any time; we shall ask you to infer that he was.'

Ainger referred to Merrill's statement to the police, and took from Wells a document from the mass of papers lying in front of him. 'Referring to his wife, Merrill said: "I think I may have suggested that she should get some arsenic from a local chemist for use in killing weeds".' Ainger glanced up at the jury. 'The Crown suggests for your consideration that Merrill may well have thought it most necessary to his plan to keep his name off the chemists' poison register. That is a matter entirely for you.'

Ainger wound up with: 'Direct evidence in a poisoning case, members of the jury, is practically impossible in a crime so sinister and subtle. But if there is no direct evidence, circumstantial evidence is valuable, if each separate part of it fits in with the rest like the parts of a puzzle, and points to one conclusion. That the prisoner had the means, the opportunity, and the motive to administer poison to Mrs. Merrill, and that he murdered her.'

First witness for the Crown was Gwladys Williams. She was dressed in her Sunday best; she said that she had been employed at Fancy for the past three years, coming there from Bangor which was her home town, a week or two after Mr. and Mrs. Merrill had arrived in Castlebay. A helper came in sometimes to do the rougher work.

Mrs. Merrill's health changed for the worse about the middle of December, 1955. Went off her food, and had things like rice puddings, what might be called invalid food.

'And did you always prepare these rice puddings,' Wells, who was taking her through her evidence, asked, 'and other food for Mrs. Merrill?'

'I did, except when the nurse arrived and she cooked some of the meals, too.'

She went on to describe Dr. Griffiths's visits, and how, after mid-December, he was constantly at Fancy; and how during the last days of her life, Merrill used to come back from the office for lunch every day. Previously he had always lunched out. She said that he sometimes sat in his wife's room, alone with her.

On the night of the dinner party when Edward Stone

and his wife were guests, Gwladys Williams described how she had prepared the food, and had waited at the table as usual.

'Have you known Mrs. Merrill ever to use any arsenic for killing weeds in the garden,' Wells asked her, 'before her death, or did Mr. Merrill?'

'I only remember Mrs. Merrill talking about weed killing with arsenic to the gardener. That was during last summer.'

'Did you see Mr. Merrill in the kitchen while the dinner to which Mr. and Mrs. Stone came was being prepared?'

'He may have come in once or twice to speak to me, but I don't remember.'

'Did he come into the kitchen while you were preparing the meal at all that evening?' Wells's tone was more probing.

Gwladys Williams scowled to herself as she tried to recall the occasion. She shook her head. 'I don't think so,' she said. 'But I was busy, I don't really remember.'

Wells knew he was on ground which might yield some profitable information; he dug away. 'Used Mr. Merrill to come into the kitchen very often?'

'Hardly ever.'

'What about when Mrs. Merrill was alive?'

'I don't remember him coming into the kitchen then.'

'What about when she was ill? Did Mr. Merrill come into the kitchen then? To give instructions about her food for instance?'

'He may have come once or twice; but it was mostly

Dr. Griffiths or the nurse who spoke to me about Mrs. Merrill's meals.'

'Did Mr. Merrill ever cook any of his wife's meals?'

'I never remember him doing so.'

'Did you ever see any arsenic in the bedroom?'

'Not that I know of; I didn't see any.'

'And you did not give her any by mistake?'

'Not likely. I gave her just her food, sometimes the medicine the doctor said she was to take.'

Wells turned to mutter to Ainger, who nodded. Wells looked at the judge. 'My lord, may the witness, Mrs. Stone, come into court?'

'Yes, if you want her.'

A faint murmur ran round the courtroom as Margot Stone's name was called; and then she came in, hesitantly. She stood in the well of the court, in view of the dock.

Wells regarded her for a moment, everyone was staring at her, but she seemed quite self-possessed, her hair catching the light shafting through the windows.

'Miss Williams, look at her,' Wells said sharply; she was already looking. 'Have you ever seen her before?'

'Yes. I saw her at Fancy.'

'When was that?'

'After Mrs. Merrill died.'

'Do you remember any particular occasion?'

'I remember seeing her and Mr. Merrill in the dining room together.'

'Did you hear anything particular said?'

'Yes, I heard him say: "Why don't you leave him"?'

'And did you hear any reply?'

'Yes, I heard her say: "I can't do that, Dick, much as I love you".'

'Anything else?'

'That was all I heard.'

Wells threw an inquiring glance at Ainger as he sat down as if to say he had made a start; and while Margot Stone went out of the courtroom, Harry Deveen got to his feet to cross-examine.

'Miss Williams, you saw Mrs. Merrill every day during her illness?'

'Yes, I did.'

'Did she ever seem depressed?'

'Yes, she did, so would anyone. She was that ill.'

'All I asked you was whether Mrs. Merrill seemed depressed?' Gwladys Williams nodded. 'Was she well enough to get out of bed sometimes?'

'She got out of bed sometimes when I was present, but I can't speak of the times when I wasn't there.'

'So she might have got out of bed when you weren't there?'

'She might, of course, but I shouldn't say it was likely.'

'Now, about Mrs. Stone. You have spoken of a particular occasion in the dining room?'

'Yes.'

'Did you go into the room.'

'No, I didn't.'

'So you may be mistaken when you say it was Mrs. Stone?'

'No mistake at all.'

'If you didn't go into the room, you didn't in fact see Mrs. Stone or anybody else?'

'Oh, yes, I did. I went into the room to speak to Mr. Merrill. I didn't know there was anyone else there. I opened the door and as soon as I saw Mrs. Stone, I closed it again.'

'You are certain you opened the door long enough to be sure it was Mrs. Stone?'

'Quite long enough.'

'Isn't it rather remarkable that at the very moment you should open the door, Merrill was asking Mrs. Stone, if it was her, to leave her husband?'

'Well, that's what happened anyway.'

'You don't think you may have dreamt this?'

'Not likely. I was very shocked at what was going on.'

'You don't like Mr. Merrill?'

'Not after I knew he was carrying on with Mrs. Stone, I didn't.'

'Thank you, Miss Williams.'

Gwladys Williams stood there hesitantly, looking somewhat self-righteous, before the usher indicated to her to leave the witness box. Mr. Justice Lane adjourned until the following morning and the court rose for the day, and the telephones to London got busy.

Margot Stone's unexpected appearance in court had added a nice touch of drama to the proceedings.

CHAPTER ELEVEN

Next morning, the prosecution called Nurse Howells who described herself as a professionally trained nurse who lived in Rhyl. Thin-faced, spinsterish, she had come to Fancy as the result of a phone call from Richard Merrill on 16th January, 1956.

She began by describing how ill Mrs. Merrill was. 'During the last four days of her life I used to feed her myself. She was so ill she was not able to manage to do so herself; she wasn't able to get out of bed.'

'Was the use of her legs in any way affected or not?' It was Ainger who was taking her through her examination-in-chief.

'She seemed to be more or less paralysed; she couldn't move her feet, or her hands very much.'

'Did Merrill come into her bedroom frequently during this time?'

'When he was at home, yes; but he was out a great deal during the day at the office. He came back for lunch.'

'When he came back from the office for lunch, used he to go upstairs to the bedroom?'

'That was the first thing he did, to see how his wife

was.'

'Mr. and Mrs. Merrill occupied separate bedrooms?'

'Yes,' Nurse Howells said; 'since Mrs. Merrill's illness; it was her idea.'

Nurse Howells gave an account of the last days of Mrs. Merrill's illness, how she ceased to have anything except invalid food, a little milk, sometimes soda-water and milk.

'And all these invalid foods, the milk and so on were prepared in the kitchen?'

'Yes, sometimes I prepared it, sometimes Gwladys Williams.'

'Did Mr. Merrill ever prepare his wife's food?'

'I don't remember that.'

'Was he ever in the bedroom when she was having her food?'

'Oh, yes, of course, he would often stay and coax her to take something.'

'Do you remember,' and Ainger's quiet tones took on an unmistakable edge, 'Merrill ever being left in the bedroom alone with his wife, coaxing her to take a little of the food you had prepared for her?'

'He might have done; I can't remember any partic-ular time. But, of course, he was her husband, and he seemed very affectionate and very anxious about her illness.'

But Ainger wasn't going to let one of the prosecu-tor's own witnesses leave it there. 'But presumably you couldn't have seen Mrs. Merrill every mealtime. What about when you yourself had a meal?'

'I used to go downstairs for my meals, of course. I usually had them with Gwladys Williams in the kitchen.'

Ainger nodded with shrewd understanding. 'Naturally you had to keep yourself strong and capable of performing the duties required of you. And so you had to have your meals and your rest.'

'I didn't get much rest the night Mrs. Merrill died.'

'I am coming to that,' Ainger said suavely. 'But first I want to ask you if, to your knowledge, Merrill ever gave his wife her food?'

'Sometimes, yes. Sometimes Gwladys Williams did.'

'To continue with Mrs. Merrill's illness, when did the attacks of sickness occur?'

'The vomiting always occurred after she took food.'

'And did this vomiting continue?'

'From 19th January on until her death. By now her legs and arms were wasting very much. The skin, I noticed was going very dark and copper-coloured.'

'Did she show any desire for food?'

'Yes, she was very anxious to get better. She made attempts to keep the food down.'

She described how on the day of Mrs. Merrill's death, in the early hours about 4 a.m. she noticed a change in her condition. She did not rouse Merrill or send any message to him until about eight o'clock. Mrs. Merrill was then quite conscious.

At eight a.m. on 21st January, Nurse Howells called Merrill, who at once came in to see his wife. 'The doctor, I think, came about 9:30 a.m. I cannot remember whether Mr. Merrill was present then or not.'

When Merrill came into the room, Nurse Howells said, Mrs. Merrill spoke to him, but what passed between them she did not know. Mrs. Merrill was then very weak; she was on the point of dying. 'I realized she was much weaker, and there was really no chance. She died at ten a.m.'

Ainger sat down. There was a slight pause, during the heavy silence, a juror scraped his foot on the wooden floor and the sound brought glances round to him. Then Harry Deveen got to his feet to cross-examine.

He began by suggesting to the jury that Mrs. Merrill, far from having had arsenic administered to her by her husband, might have taken it herself.

'If Mrs. Merrill could have got out of bed during the last days of her illness,' he said to Nurse Howells, 'she could have got hold of arsenic herself and taken it. You said at the magistrates' court that she was not up on 19th January, but what do you say about any time during the last four days?'

'I've already said she could not even sit up in bed; she did not get out of bed during those four days to my knowledge; I don't think she could have managed it.'

There was nothing much that Deveen could do about it, and he sat down.

Ainger with a self-confident touch to his wig, stood up to say quietly to the witness: 'Did you ever find during the time you were there at the house before or after Mrs. Merrill's death, anything in the room which she might have taken to poison herself?'

'No.'

Next into the witness box, Morgan the Coffin, red-haired, with a soft voice and chirpy manner. 'The coffin was made in my workshop, and I engraved the nameplate. My son and I put the body into the coffin. The towel was placed in the coffin over the body and underneath the side. A silk-pocket-handkerchief was placed on her face. She was buried in Castlebay church-yard on 25th January 1956, in my presence.'

He had rattled it off parrot-wise, and Ainger caught him in the pause he made for breath, and questioned him about the exhumation. Morgan the Coffin shot off again.

'I was present at the Castlebay churchyard when Mrs. Merrill's body was exhumed. It was the same coffin which I had seen placed there in January, 1956. The coffin was removed to Church Cottage, near the churchyard. At 11:55 p.m. I opened the coffin in the presence of Dr. Mortlake, Dr. Griffiths, Superintendent Larrabee, Inspector Owen, and Sergeant Pitt. I saw the body; it was the body of Mrs. Merrill. The towel and the handkerchief and other things were exactly as I put them. I was present at the post-mortem examination and I subsequently replaced the body for reinternment.'

No questions.

A touch of macabre humour lightened the atmosphere of the musty courtroom, when the next witness was called, Morgan the Garden. He was Merrill's gardener, and it was obvious the moment he stepped into the box, red-haired, small, and with that same sparrow-like manner, that he was the undertaker's twin brother.

He described himself as a jobbing gardener; and he had never used any weed killer at Fancy while he had worked there, which was from the time the Merrills had taken the house.

'Mrs. Merrill never mentioned arsenic to me, nor any method of making weed killer. Fancy was a terrible place for weeds.' No, Mr. Merrill had never discussed using weed killer. Mr. Merrill didn't take much interest in the garden.

Cross-examining, Harry Deveen asked: 'You say that Fancy was a very bad place for weeds?'

'That's right, sir.'

'And you being the gardener looking after the garden, how did you cope with these weeds?'

'Pulled them out. I don't hold with these chemicals; they ruins the soil. Besides, the time you take mixing the stuff up ready to use, you might just as well pull them out.'

'You say neither Mr. or Mrs. Merrill ever suggested using weed killer to you. Did you ever mention it to Mrs. or Mr. Merrill?'

There was a slight pause; Morgan the Garden scratched his red hair with a reflective finger. 'I may have done,' he said, 'but I don't remember.'

'Even though you don't approve of the use of weed killer?'

'I don't hold with lots of things, but it doesn't mean

I can't talk about them.'

And with that Morgan the Garden took his place in the court next to Morgan the Coffin. They sat there, smiling primly at each other, while the next witness was called.

It was Edward Stone.

Edward Stone looked pretty haggard, and Ainger was using his sympathetic tone, warm and pitched to the man-of-the-world note.

'Did you, as a result of gossip that you heard, and a talk with your wife, decide to go and see Merrill?'

'Yes, I called at his office, and told him what I had heard about him and my wife.'

'What did he say?'

'He was perfectly pleasant about it; he's that type, full of charm when it suits him, and he promised he would not see my wife again.'

A pause while the barely-veiled reference to one of Merrill's most outstanding characteristics sank in. Dick Merrill sitting there upright, his pale-blue eyes bright in his tanned, classically sculptured face, gave no sign that he had caught the malice in what Stone had just said.

Ainger took his rimless pince-nez off and then replaced them. 'Later on did the accused invite you and your wife to dinner?'

'Yes, he did. We were to go to dinner with him on 6th July last.'

'And before you went did something happen?'

'I continued to hear rumours.'

'And did you go to Merrill's office again?'

'Yes.'

'And what happened?'

'He admitted that he had met my wife again. He said that the meeting was purely accidental, and though he had flirted with her in a harmless way, he assured me that there should be no further trouble.'

'Were you satisfied with this?'

'I was. I said I would still bring my wife to dinner as arranged. He seemed pleased at this and offered me a cup of tea. I declined this, but he pressed me to have it. I could not tell you why, but I still declined it.'

'Did Merrill have tea?'

'Yes, he drank his.'

'But you didn't touch yours?'

'No, I did not.'

Stone smiled wryly at Ainger, as if to say that it was a good thing he hadn't drunk that cup of tea which Merrill had seemed so anxious for him to drink. There was a stir of interest in court; then the next question.

'And you went to Merrill's house for dinner, you and your wife?'

'Yes, we did. Merrill was as charming as ever; I could see why my wife was attracted to him.'

'Did you see anything suspicious?'

'No, to be quite frank, I did not.'

'Did you have anything to drink with your meal?'

'We had wine. I drank very little; and we had coffee afterwards.'

'And before leaving with your wife, did you have

anything?'

'He said I should have one for the road, a brandy.'

'Did you drink it?'

'At first I declined. He was rather persuasive, so I took it.'

'And then you and your wife left?'

'Yes.'

'And soon after you got home that night, were you taken ill?'

'I was. I was terribly sick throughout the night, and in the morning my wife sent for Dr. Griffiths.'

Ainger sat down, took off his wig and replaced it on his thinning grey hair, as Deveen stood up slowly and deliberately. From his first question the line he was taking was apparent.

'Merrill is a friendly sort of person, isn't he?'

'I had nothing to complain about in that respect,' Stone said. 'My complaint was that he was too friendly with my wife.'

'And your wife is younger than you?'

'Yes, she is.'

'Do you not think you may have been unnecessarily jealous?'

'I don't think so. When I heard gossip about my wife and Merrill I thought at the time I should do something about it.'

'Gossip can be very unreliable, don't you agree, Mr. Stone?'

'I didn't think it was in this case. That's why I went to see him in the first place.'

'And he was quite nice to you about it?'

Deveen's simple, conversational way of framing his questions made them sometimes sound almost banal. Now and again he used the trick of repetition, so that the witness would pause a moment before answering, unsure whether or not that he had already replied to the question. But it could appear as if the witness was having to be careful about choosing his words before he answered.

'He wouldn't see my wife again, he said,' Stone was saying, 'but he didn't keep his word.'

'So you went to see him again?'

'Yes, he had invited us to dinner, and I thought it was right to see him again before we went.'

'And again he was quite agreeable?'

'He said it should not happen again.'

'And, in his typically friendly spirit he offered you refreshment?'

'He pressed me to have some tea, but I declined. Perhaps it was just as well for me.'

'Perhaps, Mr. Stone, but we don't know. At any rate although you declined his friendly offer of a cup of tea, you accepted his invitation to you and your wife to have dinner with him?'

'Yes.'

'You didn't think that perhaps it would be just as well if you and Mrs. Stone didn't go to dinner with him?'

'Yes. Now I wish we hadn't.'

'Why? Didn't you enjoy a pleasant evening?'

'Not as it turned out afterwards; I was most terribly ill.'

'But that was afterwards, as you say. When you had left Merrill's house?'

'I was poisoned; I was given arsenic in my drink.'

'So you say, Mr. Stone. But you don't know that Merrill poisoned you?'

'It certainly wasn't my wife. It must have been him.'

'Not necessarily; it might have been left by accident at the bottom of the glass.' Stone looked very dubious at the possibility. 'You say you did have some wine?' Deveen said.

'Yes, I did.'

'And a glass of brandy before you left?'

'Yes, he pressed it on me.'

'Maybe that was because he was a good host.'

'Maybe.'

'And you don't know where the glasses came from?'

'No, I didn't notice. Naturally I didn't know I was going to be poisoned.'

Harry Deveen eyed Stone for a moment, then he sat down; Ainger didn't re-examine.

CHAPTER TWELVE

There was nothing Philip Vane could do at Castle-bay.

Davies and Royston phoned him at his Jermyn Street flat to tell him the way the wind was blowing. He had done his job; he had rustled up the business for Royston; he had sewn-up Merrill's life story for the dirtiest Sunday newspaper for £4,000, plus a little private deal he had on with a near-pornographic paper-back publisher he knew for sexed-up, condemned cell stuff for £1,000.

If it came to that.

So there could only be one reason for him to be there. And she would be worrying about Merrill.

Vane couldn't stop himself from picturing her face if she saw him in court. But because he had chosen to work up a private obsession didn't mean she wasn't still in love with Merrill. And if he made it, she would divorce Stone and marry him.

Davies told him over the phone what she looked like when she followed Stone into the witness box. The time was pushing 3:30 p.m. The afternoon was begin-ning to lengthen the shadows.

As she took the oath, she looked across at the dock and smiled at Merrill. A shaft of light caught her hair, so that it gleamed like a golden cap.

Ainger caught the look she had exchanged with Merrill, the same way Claud Ashton had at the magistrates court; he knew what he was up against. But Ainger had felt bound to call her; she was clearly a material witness.

'Have you known the prisoner some time?' he said to her.

'I've known Mr. Merrill two years, I suppose.'

'And did you see the prisoner from time to time.'

'Just as friends, yes.'

'And you remember the dinner party when you and your husband went to dine at his house called Fancy?'

'I remember it, of course.'

She repeated the description which her husband had given of the dinner, and then she went on to describe what happened later that evening, when they got back to Tamarisk.

'It was just before we were going to bed. My husband complained that he was feeling sick, and suddenly he rushed out of the bedroom, and I heard him in the bathroom. I didn't see him actually being sick, but I could hear him, and when he came back he was a ghastly colour. Then just before he got into bed he had to go out to the bathroom again. This happened several times; he complained that his heart was beating very rapidly. In fact, he wondered if it was some sort of heart-attack, but I thought something must have upset him at dinner.'

'You yourself were perfectly all right after dinner?'

'Yes, I was perfectly all right. I gave my husband hot water to drink, but it didn't seem to have any effect, and so he took sips of brandy and water. He was in bed feeling very cold and I got him a hot water bottle. We have separate beds, and I went to bed hoping he would sleep it off, but he didn't. He kept on being sick all through the night.'

Next morning she had phoned Dr. Griffiths, who came right away.

Stone had been ill during the rest of the day; but as the result of taking Dr. Griffiths's medicine he had begun to feel better. Next day, Margot Stone said, he was up after a fair night. He was still feeling very shaky, but the sickness had stopped. Dr. Griffiths had seen him again the previous evening, and the next morning.

'Mrs. Stone, can you throw any light on the fact that after this dinner party to which you and your husband went with the prisoner, he was taken ill with arsenical poisoning?'

'How could I throw any light on it? If you are suggesting that the arsenic came from Mr. Merrill, I simply do not believe it. Ask my husband, he may know where it came from.'

Ainger pulled off his pince-nez and replaced it, and went on imperturbably.

'Now I want to ask you something else. Apart from the dinner party have you ever been to visit the house, Fancy?'

'You mean alone.'

'Alone, Mrs. Stone.'

'No, I've never been there alone. In fact the only occasion I have ever been to Fancy was the dinner party.'

Off came the pince-nez again, and Ainger tapped it against the fingers of his other hand. He slitted his eyes and peered at the witness box like some huge blackbird examining a prospective morsel of dubious flavour.

'My lord,' he rasped, 'I ask for leave to treat this witness as a hostile witness. Will your lordship be good enough to look at the deposition she gave before the magistrates' court?'

The judge pushed into the papers before him and found the deposition. He read it. 'What do you say?' he said looking at Harry Deveen.

'My lord, it is of course a matter entirely for your lord-ship, but I submit that the witness has not yet brought herself within the category of a hostile witness.'

Mr. Justice Lane was frowning at Margot Stone. 'But I have been watching her demeanour, and looked at what she said before the magistrates. Yes, I shall give you leave, Mr. Attorney.'

Ainger turned to the witness box.

'Mrs. Stone, will you take your deposition?' The Clerk of the Court handed it up; she looked at it with apparent little interest. 'Do you see your signature at the foot of the deposition?'

'Yes, I do.'

'Look at the paragraph just above it.' Ainger turned

to a copy of the deposition, which Wells had handed him and began to read from it, facing the jury. 'I have been to Fancy once or twice by myself, but I cannot remember the exact occasions.' He turned back to her. 'You told my lord and the jury a few moments ago that you had never been to Fancy alone. Which is true, what you swore here or what you swore before the justices?'

There was no answer.

Ainger repeated his question. Still she remained silent.

'Very well, Mrs. Stone,' Ainger said. 'I shall ask the jury in due course to draw their own conclusions.'

He sat down; and the case was adjourned until the next day.

CHAPTER THIRTEEN

The first witness next morning, Wednesday, 17th October, 1956, was Sergeant Parry, giving evidence of having been in charge of the specimen-jar which he had taken to Cardiff police laboratory; and this formality completed, Dr. Griffiths took Parry's place.

He had been in practice some twenty-five years. He had attended Mrs. Merrill at irregular intervals for three years for rheumatic complaints of varying intensity.

He came to 22nd December, 1955, when he was sent for by Merrill. 'I found Mrs. Merrill with a pulse of 120. A normal pulse would be about 80. She told me she had been vomiting, and she complained of pain in her stomach. She told me she was subject to these bilious attacks. There was a cyanosed condition round the lips; that indicates a failure of circulation. The skin of her abdomen was sallow.'

'Having regard to what you know now, is that an important matter?'

'It is an important matter,' Dr. Griffiths said.

'When did you next see Mrs. Merrill?'

'I continued to see her; her condition continued to

deteriorate. Then on 11th January, 1956, she complained to me of curious feelings in her feet. She described them as springs pressing her up from the ground. I took her arm and tried to get her to walk naturally round the room. She was unable to do so.'

'What conclusion did you draw from this condition?'

'I was familiar with the high-stepping walk as being a symptom of multiple neuritis,' Dr. Griffiths said. 'I helped her upstairs. When she was in bed I examined her. I tested her knee-jerks. The knee-jerks were totally absent. Absence of knee-jerks occurs in some diseases, notably multiple neuritis. I also noticed the grip of her hands. It was diminished.'

'When did you next examine Mrs. Merrill?'

Dr. Griffiths referred to his notes. 'The next time I visited her was on 16th January. When I arrived, she was in bed. Mr. Merrill told me she had been vomiting. She complained of pain over the abdomen. I examined the abdomen. There was no distention; it was rather retracted; no acute abdominal condition in the sense of appendicitis or peritonitis. There was no enlargement of the liver, and I examined her heart, and there was a mitral systolic-murmur there; its action was rapid, and her pulse was 120. Her lips were cyanosed, blue, and it was now that I noticed the discoloration of the skin. I examined her urine, and I found there was albumen in it, which indicated some disturbance of the function of the kidneys. I made up a bottle of medicine for her, useful in certain forms of bilious vomiting.'

'From anything she said to you,' the judge said, 'or

from anything said to you by anybody else, or anything you observed, did you suspect that she might take her own life?'

Dr. Griffiths looked at him as if he hadn't heard the question properly, then he said: 'I did not.'

'When did you next see Mrs. Merrill?' Ainger asked.

'On 17th January at three p.m., and again at 10:30 p.m. She was in great pain, and in the evening I gave her a hypodermic injection to help her to sleep, and also to relieve the acute abdominal pain she was suffering from. She was very acutely ill, and vomiting everything that I attempted to give her. From 17th January I was visiting her every day. I saw her again on 20th January; she was much weaker. She was not able to retain any food. Mr. Merrill had engaged a nurse; she had arrived some days before.'

'She was keeping a proper report of all this, of course?' the judge said.

'Yes. I had to tell Mr. Merrill,' Dr. Griffiths continued, 'I think on the Friday: there was nothing to be done for her, and that she would die. I was out on the early morning of 21st January; it was a confinement. When I got back at about nine o'clock, I found a telephone message from Mr. Merrill. When I arrived at the house, Mrs. Merrill was unconscious. Mr. Merrill was in the room, and I told him what I expected would happen. I said she would not regain consciousness; she might last the day out, but I could not tell. Later that morning, about midday, Mr. Merrill phoned to say that his wife was dead. I went along at once and I gave a certificate.'

'Dr. Griffiths,' Ainger said, 'was Mrs. Merrill able to leave her bed towards the latter part of her illness?'

'While I was visiting Mrs. Merrill from 16th January every day onwards to 21st January, she was not able to get out of bed. The nurse, of course, had better knowledge than I, but from my own knowledge of her condition I do not think she could have moved her legs at all during the last four days. Nor do I think she could have fed herself during the last four days, but she certainly could not lift herself.'

'What did you put in the certificate of death? Just look at it.'

Dr. Griffiths took the certificate which the clerk passed to him.

'Yes,' he said, looming up at Ainger, 'this is the certificate that I gave to the effect that death was due to heart disease, and the period I gave for it was twelve months; nephritis, that is Bright's Disease, inflammation of the kidneys, six months; and acute gastritis, twenty-one days. At that time my opinion was that the acute gastritis was caused by toxaemia, that is to say, a collection of poisons in the blood due to inefficient kidney action, and that the Bright's Disease was secondary to the heart disease, which I put down at the time to a rheumatic condition.'

'You did not then suspect,' Ainger said, 'that poison had been introduced by somebody?'

'No.'

'As we now know it to be, arsenic was found in the

body nearly six months subsequently. What is your opinion now?'

'My opinion now is that her illness was caused by arsenical poisoning.'

'Do you mean a single dose on one day or not?'

'I should think it would be building up for several days, a week or so. The later symptoms and the acute gastritis were due to continued large doses of arsenic.'

'When you say large, what do you mean?'

'Not absolutely poisonous, but continued; perhaps a grain administered from time to time, and the fatal termination was due to an actually poisonous dose.'

'What sort of quantity?'

'Anything over two grains.'

'Supposing Mrs. Merrill had within her reach or in a cupboard in her room a bottle containing arsenic, do you think that in her condition it would be possible for her to have administered it to herself during the last three or four days of her life?'

'Absolutely impossible.'

Dr. Griffiths came to Mrs. Stone's phone call to him the morning after Merrill's dinner party. Her husband was ill with what she thought to be food poisoning. Dr. Griffiths went to Tamarisk at about ten a.m. Stone was in bed and had been vomiting incessantly all night. 'His pulse was rapid, 120. The heart sounds were normal, but a very rapid action. The normal rate of the heart for a man like Mr. Stone is 76 to 80.'

He decided he was suffering from a bilious attack, and prescribed accordingly. He saw Stone again in the evening, and he was still vomiting. His pulse was still rapid, but his condition was slightly better. 'I saw him on the following morning, and he was still complaining of sickness, but his pulse was less rapid. I took a sample of his urine which I took to the Castlebay police next day.'

'We know that this sample contained traces of arsenic, Dr. Griffiths. Would you expect to find that as a result of a bilious attack?'

'No. In my opinion it is not possible under any normal attack of biliousness to find arsenic in the urine; I have now formed the opinion that Mr. Stone's illness was caused by his taking a considerable dose of arsenic.'

No, he could not say what had prompted him to obtain the sample; some intuition, perhaps, which he could not pin down.

Ainger left it at that.

Harry Deveen stood up on his feet slowly, purposefully. This was the first big hurdle he had to get over; this was the first tough part. If he could turn this witness to Merrill's advantage, the case would be running well for him.

'During the whole time you were attending Mrs. Merrill, right up to and including her death, was there anything which was inconsistent with natural causes?'

'No,' Dr. Griffiths said. Otherwise he would not have given a death certificate.

'There would be nothing,' Deveen said, 'unusual in her looking pale or sallow, when she was ill at this particular time, or your attention would have been drawn to it?'

'It was quite consistent with her other symptoms, which I thought at the time were due to biliousness.'

'During this time in December, 1955, when you were attending her and she was suffering from bilious attacks,' Harry Deveen's shark-like face jutted forward, 'you did not think of some form of toxaemia, or self-poisoning, caused by some poison taken or administered?'

'No, I didn't think of that.'

'A person in such a condition perhaps for a number of years may be poisoning herself, unconsciously, of course, without realizing it?'

'Yes.'

Mr. Justice Lane leaned forward.

'A very decayed tooth may cause it?' he said.

Dr. Griffiths looked at him. 'A decayed tooth could, over a length of time, set up toxaemia.'

'Or continued indigestion, or continued rheumatism,' Deveen said, 'that is right, is it not, Dr. Griffiths?'

'It is true that a person could suffer from toxaemia, as a result of chronic indigestion or rheumatism.'

The judge leaned forward a little further and eyed Deveen. 'Chronic indigestion or rheumatism may cause toxaemia,' he said, 'but chronic indigestion or rheumatism would not cause poisoning by arsenic.'

'With great respect, nobody is suggesting that, my lord.' Deveen turned back to

Dr. Griffiths. 'During December to January, the condition you then found, this toxaemia, may have been set up by ill-health, caused by continued indigestion and rheumatism?'

'I never thought so in Mrs. Merrill's case.'

'But do you admit,' Harry Deveen said, 'that a person suffering from continued indigestion or rheumatism may suffer from toxaemia?'

Dr. Griffiths shifted uneasily; he was trying to be honest and as fair to Merrill as he could possibly be. 'There are certain conditions that may produce acute toxaemia, but ordinary indigestion or rheumatism is not one.'

Deveen was still there, prodding away, grim and determined. Then suddenly he faced the jury and smiled faintly as if to say they were not to take all this too seriously, the local doctor was getting a little confused, but it was nothing against him Deveen turned back to the witness.

'If you found a person suffering from one or both of these different diseases, are you prepared to swear that she may not suffer from toxaemia?'

Here Mr. Justice Lane decided he'd had enough. 'The witness has already said Mrs. Merrill died from arsenical poisoning. What we're concerned with is whether she was murdered or not, not whether she died of poisoning by other means.'

Harry Deveen's expression was aggrieved, and he pointed out to the judge that he was defending a man charged with murder, and that he ought to be permitted to question the witness on all the matters the prosecution had raised, and they had gone into Mrs. Merrill's symptoms in some detail.

Mr. Justice Lane looked at him silently, and Deveen changed his tack; he was determined to shake Dr. Griffiths anyway, and he continued with questions about Dr. Griffiths's further visits towards the end of Mrs. Merrill's illness.

'I went to see Mrs. Merrill on 11th January, 1956,' Dr. Griffiths said. 'She complained of suffering from this tingling feeling, as she put it, in her feet. She had not got these symptoms when I had last seen her; she was perfectly able to walk.'

'So that this condition started on 11th January?'

'Yes; the high-stepping walk, which whatever the cause is, as I've said, is a symptom of multiple neuritis. Her condition did not suggest that she was danger-ously ill. I went to see her on 16th January, when I was reckoning on visiting her once a week. She had been vomiting a great deal, and from that time I never remember any improvement in her condition.'

Deveen shifted on quickly to ask Dr. Griffiths about Mrs. Merrill's ability to move about during the four days prior to her death. Dr. Griffiths was emphatic that she could not have walked after 18th January; nor, in his opinion, could she have fed herself during the last four days of her life.

He told Deveen how Merrill had sent for him on the morning of his wife's death; and then Deveen adroitly got him to Stone's illness.

Dr. Griffiths had formed the opinion that Stone's symptoms were consistent with a bilious attack, with the exception of the rapid pulse.

'It was only the fact that arsenic was found in the patient's urine that made you change your opinion?'

'That aroused my suspicions.'

'What was found was one thirty-third of a grain of arsenic?'

'That is what was reported to me.'

'There are many ways, are there not,' Harry Deveen said, 'in which a very small trace of arsenic can be found in a person's body, without that arsenic having been wilfully administered?'

'There are ways, yes,' Dr. Griffiths said.

'And there are a number of medicines that do in fact contain some minute quantities of arsenic?'

'There are.'

'One thirty-third of a grain, if that were all, would not affect a person at all?'

'No.'

Harry Deveen glanced at the jury again, as if to say that he'd got precisely what he wanted from the witness and he was very well satisfied with the results of his efforts. The jury looked unimpressed; they knew and respected Dr. Griffiths, as their fathers and mothers had before them known his father, and no slick lawyer was going to shift their loyalty.

Deveen had finished with Dr. Griffiths, but Ainger returned to the attack. 'Dr. Griffiths, I want to come back to Mrs. Merrill's multiple neuritis. If poison is the cause of multiple neuritis, must it be acute or not?'

'It must be acute.'

'Now, on 11th January, 1956, was that the date on which the high-stepping walk occurred?'

'Yes.'

'Will you give us your opinion of what her condition was on that date?'

'On 11th January, 1956,' Dr. Griffiths said, 'she was suffering from multiple neuritis.'

Ainger gave him a nod and he left the witness box. Dr. Griffiths kept his eyes averted from the dock.

Dark, middle-aged, sharp-featured Pryce the Chemist was next, and he gave the date nearly three months before her death when Mrs. Merrill had bought a quarter of a pound of arsenic from him; she said she wanted it for weed-killing.

The poison book was brought, and Pryce riffled through the pages, stiff and crackling in the musty silence of the court, until he came to the page that showed that Mrs. Merrill had bought a quarter of a pound of arsenic.

'That's Mrs. Merrill's signature.'

The Attorney-General now brought him up to 8th July last, when Dr. Griffiths had asked him to let him have a clean bottle for the purpose of conveying a urine specimen away for analysis.

'I selected a clean bottle,' Pryce said in his precise tones, 'washed it thoroughly and took it to Dr. Griffiths. He brought the bottle back himself with the sample in it, and sealed it in my presence with my seal. He also put a label on it.'

The usher showed him the bottle with its exhibit-label tied round its neck, and Pryce agreed that it was the bottle in question.

Cross-examined by Deveen, Pryce was certain that the only entry in his poison book at the time in question was the entry concerning the arsenic sold to Mrs. Merrill. Weed killer, Pryce said, would have been noted down in the poison book. About the specimen bottle which he had given Dr. Griffiths, he thought it had been in his possession two or three months.

What had the bottle contained, before he washed it out so thoroughly for Dr. Griffiths? Peroxide of hydrogen. It had evaporated; that was why it was empty.

Harry Deveen made a long pause and then he leaned forward.

'You are sure of this? You are sure that bottle could not have contained some poison, arsenic, for instance?'

Pryce shook his head emphatically. 'Arsenic is kept in stock cans; there are practically only two arsenic preparations which I make up myself. *Liquor arsenicalis* of the British Pharmacopoeia, and *arsenici hydrochloric.* They are kept in stock bottles.'

'Could not the bottles have got mixed up by some mistake?'

Pryce's stare was practically baleful. 'I am not unaware of my responsibilities as a qualified pharmaceutical chemist,' he said, his voice high-pitched. 'All poisons, and arsenic is a dangerous poison, are kept away in the poison cupboard. As a matter of fact, all empty bottles are kept in another room where there is a sink for washing them out.'

Harry Deveen sat down and the court adjourned for the day.

CHAPTER FOURTEEN

1.

The fourth day of the trial began with Detective-Superintendent Larrabee into the witness box to describe Merrill's arrest. He referred to Merrill's statement which he had made at the first interview and in which he emphatically denied ever having possessed any arsenic.

The Clerk of the Court read out the bit: 'I think I may have suggested that she should get some arsenic from a local chemist for use in killing weeds.'

He read out how Merrill had said that if any of the arsenic was left over, it must have been thrown away; he hadn't seen any since. He certainly had never had any either at home or at his office; and he thought his wife had bought the stuff two or three months before her death; and how he suspected that some people thought he had married her for her money; and as for Mrs. Stone, she had been no more than a friend.

The Clerk of the Court also read from Merrill's statement how his wife had suffered from depression, and he had wondered if she had taken anything to end her life. 'When she died it was obvious that she hadn't poisoned herself, because Dr. Griffiths had said she died from Bright's Disease and acute gastritis?'

According to Merrill's statement, Stone's illness completely baffled him. 'If he suffered from arsenical poisoning I've no idea where the poison came from. It certainly didn't come from me. I have no motive whatever for seeking to put an end to his life.'

That was about all that Wells, examining him, had to do with Superintendent Larrabee.

Cross-examining, Harry Deveen suggested that Merrill had given the police every possible assistance during the investigation of the case. Larrabee eyed him with a veiled look. It was an innocent enough question on the face of it, but Larrabee knew Deveen from past experience. He couldn't be too wary of him.

'I couldn't say,' he said, noncommittedly.

Deveen's eyebrows shot up. 'You couldn't say?' There was disbelief in his tone.

'No, I couldn't say,' Larrabee said imperturbably. 'He certainly did not refuse to give me any information.'

Deveen's glance conveyed to the jury that Larrabee was leaning over backwards in his attempt to be cautious. But at the same time his expression implied there really was no need to adopt the attitude with him; he was not seeking to catch the witness out.

Deveen smiled with affable encouragement at Larrabee. 'Then he has given you every possible assistance?'

Larrabee looked a little uncomfortable, but stood his

ground. 'I couldn't say that,' he said.

'But why not?'

Larrabee leant forward a little over the ledge of the witness box. 'He told me about his wife acquiring arsenic,' he said, 'but he said that he himself had never been in possession of any.'

'What's wrong with that?' Deveen's voice had sharpened.

Larrabee looked at him for a moment, but again he refused to be caught. He turned to the judge. 'My lord isn't that a matter for the jury?'

'It may be,' the judge said. 'But I think Mr. Deveen is entitled to an answer to his question if you have one.'

'Thank you, my lord,' Deveen said. 'Now, Superintendent, please attend to me. I suppose I can give you the credit of having made every possible inquiry as to whether or not the accused acquired arsenic?'

'Yes, you may.'

'And it is right, is it not, that you have no evidence that the accused purchased any arsenic in the district?'

'No.'

'Nor anywhere else?'

'No, that is correct.'

'So when the accused said he had never been in possession of arsenic, he was telling you the truth?'

'My answer to that,' Superintendent Larrabee said carefully, 'is that you are correct in assuming that I have no evidence that the accused ever bought any arsenic. But we also have information that Mr. Stone, to the best of my knowledge, was never in possession of arsenic. It was not he, then, who produced arsenic at the dinner table, nor as far as I know, did Mrs. Stone.'

'So with you it is a matter of excluding Mr. and Mrs. Stone from all suspicion, and leaving the accused to bear the blame?'

Ainger hadn't the slightest intention of allowing Deveen to get away with that one. 'My lord,' he said, 'is it for the witness to argue the case for the Crown?'

'No, Mr. Attorney, but I do not like in any way to appear to hamper the defence unnecessarily.' Mr. Justice Lang looked down his long nose at Deveen: 'Have you got all you want from this witness? Superintendent Larrabee says quite frankly that he had got no evidence that the accused acquired any arsenic.'

'Very good, my lord, I will leave the matter.'

Next into the witness box Detective-Sergeant Pitt, followed by Inspector Owen and Sergeant Parry, their evidence all corroborating Superintendent Larrabee.

As the day's proceedings drew to an end Richards from Cardiff police laboratory gave evidence. 'In the case of Mr. Stone, what did you find?' Ainger asked him.

'I found about seven-tenths of a grain of arsenic.'

'Was that in the specimen you examined?'

'It was.'

'Can you tell us about how much Mr. Stone had taken?'

'No, I cannot. But I should say probably considerably more than was shown in the specimen I analysed.'

Harry Deveen had nothing to ask him; that was all for the day.

2.

Next morning Dr. Henry Mortlake went into the witness box.

According to Davies, phoning Philip Vane later, the previous day's evidence had really been the build-up to the prosecution's big gun.

Vane pictured Mortlake looking more than anything else in the world like one of the local farmers, with his powerful shoulders and open sunburnt face; you wouldn't have suspected that this was the great Mortlake.

Vane had first met him during a murder case where he had been representing the accused, and he'd found Mortlake at a mortuary in an old churchyard in the East End. Through a door marked Private, Doctors Only, was the post-mortem room.

Mortlake was wearing a white P.M. gown, rubber apron, rubber gloves, and white rubber galoshes, and he was holding a knife. He introduced Vane to a small man who was swabbing with a large sponge the interior of a body which lay on a gleaming white porcelain table; this was the mortuary-keeper.

Vane had watched while Mortlake dissected the organs on a small wooden mobile table. He had always visualized him as some sinister, mysterious figure, dodging from shadow to shadow with his bag of autopsy instruments.

The mortuary-keeper washed and tidied things up as the work progressed. Everything in the place was very clean; you got accustomed to the mingled odour of dead bodies and disinfectant. But Vane disliked the sound of the saw opening a skull. Otherwise it was devoid of anything gruesome.

After that Vane used to see him at the Old Bailey, always bluff and sunburned, rough almost and with glacial calm. There were no flies on him. He dominated the court, even the judge seemed to give place to him. Privately, Vane felt he was allowed to throw his weight about a bit too much; Vane didn't hold with his infallibility to the extent that the court did.

But he was a great performer in the witness box. In his quiet voice, with marvellous clarity, his evidence at once assumed enormous authority. As he got going that morning Vane could imagine how the chances of Dick Merrill getting away with it must have appeared pretty slim to the jury.

Come to think, to Merrill himself.

Mortlake described the exhumation at the little church in Castlebay; the body, after six months' burial, was unusually well preserved, particularly the liver and kidneys, indicative of poisonous arsenic doses being present. He could find no evidence in these organs of any natural disease such as Bright's Disease that would account for vomiting and death.

'From the amount present in the small and large intestine it is clear that a large dose of arsenic must have been taken, possibly a fatal dose, certainly within twenty-four hours of death. And from the amount of arsenic which I found in the liver, over two grains, and its condition, arsenic must have been given in large doses for some days, probably not less than a week.'

Finally, Mortlake gave it as his opinion that Stone's illness was also due to acute arsenical poisoning. The amount of arsenic found in Stone's urine sample could not be produced in any normal way.

Harry Deveen's cross-examination took as long as Ainger's examination-in-chief; it built up to an attempt to shake Mortlake's assertion that Mrs. Merrill had taken a fatal dose of arsenic less than twenty-four hours before death. Deveen quoted cases of persons who had lived for seven or eight days after taking large doses.

'Could not intermittent vomiting which subsided, and then was followed thirty-six hours later by renewed attacks be the result of arsenic becoming lodged, encapsuled, is I believe the technical term, in the stomach?'

'I have known of such cases,' Mortlake said, 'when the action of the arsenic was delayed, through becoming encapsuled in the stomach. When it was freed, death ensued very rapidly.'

Mr. Justice Lane leaned forward and wanted to know what precisely was meant by encapsuled.

Mortlake explained to him that it was possible for a dose of poison, arsenic for example, to become enclosed temporarily in a fold of the stomach lining, so that its effect would not be spread to the system, until the poison became released from its position.

'Then you would not like to exclude that someone

might take a large dose of arsenic on Monday,' Deveen said to Mortlake, 'suffer from vomiting, sickness, and so on, on Tuesday, Wednesday, and Thursday, which would then abate for say thirty-six hours, and then come on again?'

Mortlake's stubby finger and thumb rubbed his chin. 'I cannot agree to three days' sickness from a single dose, abating due to the arsenic becoming encapsuled in the stomach, and then recurring. I do not think it would do so.'

'Two days?'

'I doubt that very much indeed.'

'Do you insist then, Dr. Mortlake,' Deveen pressed him, 'that despite the possibility of the arsenic from which Mrs. Merrill died having been taken more than twenty hours previously, that all the symptoms are due to arsenical poisoning alone?'

'Of course I do.'

Mortlake's sharpened tone was a reminder that he had been saying nothing else, and that Deveen was not going to argue him out of his opinion. Deveen continued to labour the point that there could have been some other cause for the symptoms besides arsenic.

But at the end of it all Mortlake left the witness box, with his opinion that arsenical poisoning was the cause of illness in the case of both Mrs. Merrill and Stone, completely unshaken.

Harry Deveen had failed to outshoot the big gun.

Kilrain, senior official analyst to the Home Office and a pathological chemist at St. Elspeth's Hospital, was next. He described how he had received a dozen jars, the contents of which he analysed, containing portions of a body, and the others contained sawdust and shavings, and some soil.

It made fairly macabre listening.

'Jar No. 5,' he read out from his notes, in a precise clipped voice. 'This was labelled: Re E. Merrill (deceased) RM. examination. This contained a liver, which weighed 27¾ ounces. Jar No. 8. This was labelled: Re E. Merrill (deceased) RM. examination, left lung and heart. This contained a lung weighing 5½ ounces, and a heart weighing 4½ ounces.'

He had examined the contents of all those jars, he said, testing them to see if arsenic was present in all the organs, and in the fluids from the body. He had prepared a table of the arsenic he found.

'The amounts of arsenic found by me in the various organs were as follows: stomach 2.5 milligrams; stomach contents, 2.0 milligrams; jejunum and contents, 1.6 milligrams; ileum and contents, 9.1 milligrams; caecum, ascending colon and contents, 37.6 milligrams. That means a little over half-a-grain. In the liver I found over two grains. In the spleen I found one milligram. In each of both kidneys I found over one-fifth of a grain.'

The total was 3.21 grains. In the wood-shavings and in the sawdust, in the turf and soil from the bottom of the grave, he had found about one-hundredth of a grain.

He paused for a moment, before he proceeded, in his

matter-of-fact tones: 'Over the past ten years, I should think I have made analyses of 300 to 400 bodies. In every poison case, arsenic is always carefully tested for.'

'In all your vast experience,' Ainger said humourlessly, 'have you ever found a larger quantity of arsenic than you did in the organs of Mrs. Merrill's body?'

Kilrain shook his head. 'This is the largest amount of arsenic I have found in any single case of arsenical poisoning. I do not have the jars present in court,' he said in a regretful tone, 'they are still at St. Elspeth's Hospital, but I have here with me a little tube which shows the equivalent to the total amount of arsenic found in the organs named, 3.21 grains.'

The little tube glinted in the light slanting through the grimed windows. Kilrain eyed it affectionately. 'That is the amount,' he said, 'which I actually found in the body. The amount Mrs. Merrill must have taken would have been very much larger.'

'From your experience you can tell me whether that 3.21 grains would be a fatal dose?'

'Two grains is a possible fatal dose. That was the amount found in the liver alone.'

'From your experience, if the whole of the body had been submitted to you, do you think you would have found even more arsenic?'

'Undoubtedly I do.'

'As I understand it, then somebody or other gave Mrs. Merrill arsenic?'

Harry Deveen stood up quickly. 'Or she took it,' he

snapped out.

Ainger waited for Deveen to sit down again, then he proceeded to Stone's illness. Kilrain said: 'I have tested the urine and I found one thirty-third of a grain in the amount sent to me.'

'Is that what you would call a mere trace, or is it an appreciable quantity?'

'It is a good deal more than a trace; it is an appreciable quantity.'

'Is there any possible contamination of arsenic in peroxide of hydrogen?'

Again that decisive shake of Kilrain's head. 'In fact,' he said, 'a bottle that had contained peroxide of hydrogen would be an extremely good bottle to choose, because hydrogen would clean the bottle very well. You could not choose a better bottle, having rinsed it out. In my experience one would not find arsenic in urine, unless arsenic had been actually administered.'

This was the end of the examination-in-chief, Mr. Justice Lane looked at the clock which said ten minutes past four, and called it a day.

CHAPTER FIFTEEN

Saturday morning, 20th October, 1956, opened with Harry Deveen on his feet cross-examining Kilrain.

'You were asked if you would find arsenic in urine unless it was administered, or was in the bottle into which it was put before you tested it?'

'Yes.'

'Am I right in saying that arsenic is one of the generally occurring impurities in peroxide of hydrogen?'

'No, I should not expect to find it.'

'I do not ask you if you would expect to find it,' Deveen said, 'but am I right in saying that you might find it?'

'*You* might,' Kilrain said, emphasizing the word 'you'. Deveen had got all he could out of the witness, and it didn't amount to much.

Now came the prosecution's last witness, Sir Martin Wiltshire, who began by impressively listing his qualifications and experience in cases of arsenical poisoning, extending over about eighteen years.

'I have been engaged constantly in cases where it has been suggested that death was due to poisoning; in particular I have had a number of arsenical cases.'

'Is it easy or not,' Ainger asked him, 'to diagnose arsenical poisoning during life?'

'It is very difficult unless an analysis is made; the symptoms of arsenical poisoning may be imitated by actual disease. Dr. Griffiths found Mrs. Merrill physically very much better until the high-stepping walk symptom, which is the most important symptom of peripheral neuritis. Owing to the weakness of the feet, the patient lifts them high to prevent the toes catching the ground.'

'We know that from 11th January, 1956, she suffered from severe sickness, a very high pulse and systolic murmur, some indication of heart trouble. To what do you attribute those symptoms?'

'Arsenical poisoning. On 11th January there were symptoms of acute latent poison, and those indicate that arsenic was taken within a few hours of the onset of those symptoms.'

'And from and after that time the continued sickness and so on, what do they indicate to your mind?'

'Taking further large doses of arsenic.'

'When?' the judge said.

'It is impossible to say, my lord, though certainly some must have been taken within a few hours of the onset of the symptoms on 11th January.'

Mr. Justice Lane nodded and scribbled down a note. Wiltshire turned back to Ainger. 'Having regard to the analysis of the organs of the body taken six months after burial,' he said, 'I have no doubt that a possibly fatal dose was taken within twenty-four hours of death.'

'What would you say was a fatal dose?'

'By a fatal dose I mean two grains, usually accepted as a possibly fatal dose.'

'At some time during the case it was suggested that Mrs. Merrill might have committed suicide. Do you think that the taking of arsenic over a considerable period of time such as that you have told us of, would be consistent with suicide?'

'In suicide one would expect a large dose to be taken, or possibly two; in this case there were successive doses causing very painful symptoms, not in the least indicative of suicide. Rather the contrary.'

'You say many doses were taken over a long time?'

'There must have been several doses taken from 11th January to 21st January, in the last acute stage of illness.'

'Do you think that Mrs. Merrill could possibly have taken that arsenic herself?'

'I do not.'

'Not within the last twenty-four hours?'

'No; for the last four or five days it would have been impossible.'

Ainger finished up his examination with questions about Stone's illness. Wiltshire came up with the same unequivocal answers.

The symptoms pointed to some irritant poisoning inflaming the stomach and the intestines after the illness began; one thirty-third of a grain of arsenic was found in the urine passed; the illness was due to a dose of at least two grains of arsenic being taken within a very short time of the onset of the symptoms.

'What amount of arsenic,' Ainger said, 'must have been taken four days previously, if you find one thirty-third of a grain in the urine?'

'Probably over three grains.'

'Would the vomiting get rid of a considerable part of the arsenic,' the judge said, 'so that you would find less in the urine than if he had not vomited?'

'Yes, my lord.'

Harry Deveen stood up and began his cross-examination. 'What is the largest dose of arsenic which is given properly as medicine?'

'In certain diseases you may give fairly large doses. The pharmacopoeial dose goes up to eight hundredths of a grain three times a day. That is the maximum dose. That is a total of twenty-four hundredths of a grain. You can work up to that quantity three times a day, but if you give it straight away it would make the patient ill.'

'In Mr. Stone's case, as I understand it, if you had not got the analysis of the urine, the symptoms were the symptoms of ordinary gastric enteritis?'

'They might have been due to a number of causes.'

Deveen turned to the evidence of Dr. Mortlake and Kilrain in an effort to get Wiltshire to throw doubt on it. It might have seemed only hair-splitting stuff, but Deveen hadn't wasted his time; he had been leading up to the last questions he put.

'In the case of suicide by arsenic you said that you would expect one or two doses would be the most that would be taken?'

'That is rather a matter of common sense.'

Deveen stared at the witness for a moment. Then he glanced at the jury as if inviting them to listen to something of special importance which he was about to say.

'A matter of common sense? Which would be bound to depend upon the person who is taking it, does it not? A sane person would suffer such pain from the first dose, that he would not take another?'

'Yes.'

'On the other hand, someone who is not normal, might she not take two or three doses?'

This was his favourite trick, to switch to the feminine gender when he wanted to focus the jury's attention upon Mrs. Merrill.

'In order to commit suicide?' Wiltshire looked sceptical.

'What would hold with a sane person would not hold with a woman who was insane?'

'A person who threw himself out of the window and was not killed might do it again and again until he did kill himself.'

'Or,' Harry Deveen said, 'she might go to a higher window the second time?'

'No,' the judge said, 'that would show sanity.'

If Mr. Justice Lane was trying to be funny, he failed to arouse a glimmer of amusement from anyone. Perhaps he wasn't trying to be funny anyway. 'You thoroughly understood what is being put to you by

Mr. Deveen,' he said to Wiltshire, 'regarding the last hours of the life of Mrs. Merrill, and what might have happened during that time?'

'Perfectly, my lord.'

'Is suicide, then, in your opinion, a possible way to account for Mrs. Merrill's death?'

'Quite impossible;' and Wiltshire left the witness box.

'May it please your lordship, members of the jury,' Harry Deveen got to his feet again and said, 'at last I have an opportunity of addressing you who are trying Richard Merrill for his life. For a week now you have listened to the case against him, this man whom the prosecution seek to show is responsible for his wife's death. You have heard the evidence-in-chief, and you have heard the cross-examination of the witnesses, and now I hope to be able to show you that the prosecution's case is absolutely nonexistent.'

He pointed out that when a prosecution is conducted by the Crown no expense is spared in unearthing all the evidence that may help its case; the greatest medical experts are called in on its side. Whereas the accused has often only his own resources; he must fashion a defence for himself as best he can.

'He is not able to employ, for example, Dr. Mortlake,' Deveen said, 'he employs the best experts his pocket can afford; these are the witnesses that I am going to bring before you later, and they will not mind if I tell you this, they are not the greatest experts, but they will do their best to help an innocent man prove his innocence.'

Harry Deveen rocked to and fro on his heels for a few moments and then leaned forward to the jury confidentially, his expression that of a man who bore an almost unendurable weight of worry.

'I have often wondered,' he said, 'but never more have I wondered than during this last week, whether you realize the dread responsibility which rests upon the shoulders of counsel when he is defending a man for his life. It is a responsibility which I realize to the very uttermost at this moment now, as I set out to help you understand the truth in the case of Richard Merrill; and understand the truth you must, for you are to decide his innocence, or guilt.'

He began by outlining the case for the Crown, building it up in detail and then finally he said: 'But they are unable to make any suggestion at all, I have been waiting to hear it, how Merrill is supposed to have administered the poison, or the times when he was administering it. Moreover, they have failed utterly to explain to you why he should do this dreadful thing? No motive of any kind; they can offer you no more reason why Merrill should have murdered his wife than any other person in that house.'

It was for the prosecution to prove the facts, he reminded the jury, not the defence; and he suggested that the case that Mrs. Merrill took arsenic herself was infinitely stronger than the case made against her husband.

'Look at Richard Merrill, with his business integrity, his popularity in the town where he lived, happily married to his wife with whom, the whole of the evidence shows, he was living on terms of friendship and fondness right up to her death; against whom nothing was ever whispered until Dr. Griffiths went to the police with his suspicions.'

He dealt with the multiple neuritis, from which Mrs. Merrill had been suffering. While multiple neuritis may be caused by arsenical poisoning, it was equally likely to be caused by toxaemia, he argued, poisoning from within oneself, because some organ or organs of our body is not acting properly. This was what Mrs. Merrill was suffering from: multiple neuritis, caused by toxaemia.

He came to 22nd December, 1955, when Merrill sent for Dr. Griffiths. 'This man,' Deveen pointed at the dock, 'who is alleged to be poisoning his wife, sent for her doctor. That is a good start in a poison case, isn't it? Her illness does not improve, however, and gradually Mrs. Merrill is sinking; undoubtedly from 11th January, 1956 up to 21st January, the poor woman draws nearer and nearer to her death.'

Deveen looked at the jury, then at Mr. Justice Lane, then back at the jury, with an air of incredulity. 'Every day,' he said, 'I do not know when—you have to guess that, you have to guess how—but every day it is suggested that Merrill is poisoning his wife, right up to 21st January.'

He shook his head, as if the suggestion was too ludicrous to be considered. 'Now,' he said, his tone becoming serious once more, 'when I asked Dr. Mortlake, the prosecution's expert witness, about arsenic after becoming encapsuled, as it is called, in the stomach, I said would he expect to find traces of arsenic in such a case in the intestine several days after it had been taken. Dr. Mortlake said he would. As you will hear from the doctors I am going to call, arsenic can be retained in this way and gradually release itself, when you would get traces of arsenic such as were found in Mrs. Merrill. Isn't this precisely what happened in Mrs. Merrill's case? Isn't this the truth, more convincing than the prosecution's theory that this poor woman's husband, for no reason, at a time they cannot name, in a way they cannot suggest, deliberately poisoned her?'

He came to Stone's illness. Everybody had agreed, he said, Dr. Mortlake and Dr. Griffiths, that the symptoms in this case were consistent with food poisoning, except for some suspicion that depended on one-third of a grain of arsenic found in the urine.

Merrill, Harry Deveen pointed out, was not being tried for attempting to poison Stone; this was just an extra piece of evidence supposed to throw light on whether he had murdered his wife six months before. The evidence that Stone and his wife had dinner with Merrill on the night in question, and that after Stone and his wife had returned home, he was sick for the first time.

'Mrs. Stone was not sick, no one else was sick, does that prove there was arsenic in Stone's food or drink that night? Even if he had eaten or drunk something with arsenic in it, you have to be satisfied that Merrill put it there. For what motive? The fantastic motive the prosecution puts forward that he murdered his wife so that he might at some future time marry Mrs. Stone, after he had murdered her husband as well?'

Again that look of incredulity across his face, as Deveen spread out his hands. 'Of course, members of the jury, it has occurred to you, though it has not occurred to the prosecution—but we cannot expect them to think of everything—that if Merrill wanted to rid himself of his wife in order to marry Mrs. Stone, it could all have been arranged in a perfectly legal way. Through the Divorce Court. In fact, there is no evidence that this was what Merrill wanted for one moment. Even the prosecution admits there is no proof that he led an unhappy married life; they can find nothing against him at all to support their one and only motive for him murdering his wife, and attempting to murder another woman's husband.'

Deveen pointed to the empty witness box and lowered his voice to a compellingly conversational level.

'Do not forget that when Richard Merrill stands there and tells you his own true story it will be a matter of life or death for him. Do not forget that every word he says will be questioned; he will be cross-examined, fairly and properly cross-examined, by the Attorney General himself. Remember that when Merrill gives his evidence. When you have heard it, as well as the evidence which will be given by the other witnesses, you will come face to face with this vital fact. That there is no evidence that Merrill, of all people, poisoned his wife.'

He paused, his shark-like face jutting forward, for the build-up. 'It is not for him to prove that Mrs. Merrill took that poison herself. It is for the prosecution to prove beyond reasonable doubt that he poisoned her. If they have not done that, then upon all the facts that have been proved before you, both for the prosecution and for the defence, the Crown have failed in their case against Richard Merrill, and you will say that he is not guilty of murder.'

The whole atmosphere in court had changed; without any apparent effort or any special skill, Harry Deveen had suddenly made the case against Richard Merrill appear flimsy and weak.

On this curiously buoyant note Mr. Justice Lane adjourned until next Monday.

CHAPTER SIXTEEN

1.

Philip Vane learned all about the switch the trial had taken when he arrived at Caernarvon on Saturday afternoon.

Leaving London early that morning, he had driven up filled with a kind of obsessive concentration as if competing in a rally, and with a constricted feeling underneath his heart. He didn't enjoy driving this way. He liked to be relaxed.

He went to see Royston at the Caernarvon Arms, where all the lawyers were staying during the trial. Mr. Justice Lane was staying with a local V.I.P. outside the town.

Vane had tried to kid himself that it would be a good idea to have a chat with Royston about Merrill's prospects, after all hadn't he a vested interest in the outcome of the trial? The confessions of a guilty man would be more appealing to the newspaper and the paperback readers, than if he got the verdict.

Vane had tried to kid himself that it wasn't because he wanted more than he had ever wanted anything in the world to see Margot Stone. Not that, anyway, he needed to be told how tricky it would be trying to talk to her. She was a witness in the case, and it would be almost impossible for him to reach her without her husband knowing.

Royston was having his after-lunch coffee when Vane found him.

He was surprised to see Vane, who gave him a glib answer about what he was doing up there. Yes, Dick Merrill's future looked pretty rosy, Royston assured him. Deveen's speech that morning had transformed the atmosphere of the court. The jury had got all weekend to mull it over, and whichever way they listened to its echoes ringing in their ears it would still sound powerful, impregnable stuff.

Vane left Royston, who went off to join Deveen and Ainger and some of the others in the Bar Mess, a room on the first floor set apart for the lawyers, and where any tension and professional acrimony was forgotten, all were the best of friends.

Vane drove to Castlebay, he would stay there overnight, he thought. He might find Davies and learn how it looked to him. He gave the idea of telephoning Dr. Griffiths some brief thought. But it wasn't Dr. Griffiths he wanted to see, and it wouldn't get him anywhere talking to him.

He couldn't help slowing his car as Tamarisk came into view. He hadn't remembered the road at all on the way from Caernarvon, he could have run down an elephant, he told himself, and he wouldn't have noticed.

The constriction right there under his heart intensified as he glimpsed the white Jag there, outside the front door of the white-pillared portico of the large, bungalow-style house.

When he got to the hotel at Castlebay he went straight to the telephone booth. The palm of his hand was moist as he picked up the receiver and dialled the number.

'Hello?'

It was her voice, and Vane grinned to himself. It was a lucky break that her husband hadn't answered. He would have hung up and he probably wouldn't have had the guts enough to try again. She sounded a little breathless, as if the phone ringing had taken her by surprise. He wondered where her husband was, if he was nearby; if Stone could hear his voice at the other end of the telephone.

He kept his voice low.

'Remember me? I wore a pointed beard and there was that duelling scar down the side of my face.'

He did his best to keep it flip and glib; but he could hear the tremor in his tone.

She didn't answer. He thought he caught the quick intake of breath, and something told him that she knew who it was at the other end of the telephone. So that he was alert for the odd intonation in her voice, and sensed the reason for it.

'I'm afraid you've got the wrong number,' she said.

Her husband must be near her, in the room.

Vane said quickly: 'Okay. I'll drive past at four-thirty. The same car. Try and be around.'

'Yes.'

It was a quick gasp, and then she had hung up.

The telephone booth was stifling, he could feel the perspiration at his temples; the sweat was running down from his armpits under his shirt. He came out of the telephone booth, grinning triumphantly to himself again.

They had a room for him and he went up and sprawled on the bed, his senses heavy with the weight of her, his nerves tingling with the feel of her flesh.

A little later he lay in a bath; he worked the electric-shaver over his face meticulously, scowling at himself in the mirror, making sure no stubble showed under the hard line of his jaw. And all the time it wasn't his face he saw. His eyes saw his face, but the screen of his mind was crowded with hers.

He saw the white Jag parked facing him, about two hundred yards before Tamarisk, which lay beyond the gradual curve in the road. The road was empty. She didn't smile when he pulled up alongside. Her face was tense, her voice harsh and taut.

'I thought you were dead,' she said.

'I didn't know if—' he began, but she cut in.

'You'll have to follow me. Not too close.'

He nodded.

She had kept her engine running, and she used a four-letter word as she took off the brake and crashed the gears. She was nervous as hell. The road was still empty, and he reversed swiftly and went after her. She drove fast, the road she took swung off the main road, away from Conway and up the valley. He didn't know it and the road curved and narrowed like a snake, so that it took him all his time to keep her in sight.

Over to his right lay the River Conway, and the hills and woods stretched away to the left. Then the Jag was slowing and stopped at a stone bridge. Vane pulled up behind it. There was a waterfall below, and the air was moist. It was a lonely place, and they found themselves keeping their voices low.

He was explaining why he had made no attempt to reach her again, after that first meeting. He talked quickly and plausibly, while she stared at him, her expression mocking and half-filled with disbelief. He didn't tell her it was because he was afraid she would find out about his transaction with Merrill. He hadn't wanted her to know that. If it turned out to be a condemned cell confession he wouldn't want her to know he had ever had any part of that.

He made it sound that it was because he hadn't guessed there was someone else, until he had read about the case. That was why a time like this, especially, was a time for him to stay in the background.

'And when it's all over?'

'Depends,' he said.

'You mean, on how it goes for him?'

He nodded.

She said nothing. She was close to him, her fingers were twining round his hand. He thought he could feel her trembling against him. But it might have been his own blood quickening and tensing every nerve. He slid his free hand up her waist to cup her breast. He realized she was wearing a thin sweater, similar to the one she had worn before. He knew she wasn't wearing a bra this time, either.

She pushed his hand away gently, turning to him.

'In your car,' she said. 'There's more room.'

He glanced round. A few yards behind him a track turned off from the road and ended in a clump of trees. It was shadowy and dark there. She was already getting into his car. He made to follow her, then he walked quickly to the Jag. He came back holding her ignition key out to her. She took it, smiling at him.

'You think of everything,' she said.

He reversed his car off the road, up the track and into the trees which screened them from the road. The air was tangy and silent, the shadows of the trees fell across the car. He had barely cut the engine, when in that claustrophobic darkness, Margot Stone's hands reached for him with a fierce wordless urgency.

Afterwards, he watched her from under narrowed eyelids. Her head was thrown back so that her throat glimmered white. Her eyes were closed, her shadowed face held an exhausted expression, so that he experienced a moment of pity towards her. His fingers smoothed the softness of her neck and then moved down under her sweater.

She began moaning a little, and he took his hand away. She opened her eyes and stared at him questioningly.

'I don't quite—' He broke off. 'About you and him,' he muttered.

'Do there have to be any explanations?'

He gave a shrug. She began talking, jerkily as if it was costing her a great effort to force out the words. She was talking about herself. About being a school-master's daughter, living at Richmond, and how her prettiness had given her ideas about going places. She had won a couple of beauty competitions, and after she had left school she had tried the modelling racket.

Then she had married Stone. She had seen herself as secure and not unhappy, with possibilities of a harmless romance or two. Stone's idea of living at Castlebay had not been included in her calculations. But nor had Dick Merrill.

'Will you marry him?'

'You mean when—?'

She broke off. He noticed that she did not say: 'if': so, the inference was, that she felt confident of his acquittal. He wondered if she felt equally confident of his innocence. And the question gripped his thoughts, as it already had done, how much did she know about his wife's death? It was a question, which together with one or two others that had also inevitably formed themselves in his thoughts, he could not frame.

Or dare not, for fear that she might reveal, wittingly or otherwise, the extent of her knowledge of the truth?

'I suppose so,' she was saying. 'If I didn't, it might make other people wonder why.'

'Seems an odd reason for marrying someone,' he heard himself say. He tried to sound casual, to keep out of his voice the cold jealousy that crawled through his senses. While at the same time he clutched at the implication in her words that it was not because she was in love with Merrill anymore.

She turned her face to him, that faintly mocking expression on it, while her gaze travelled down from his eyes to his mouth. 'We're talking too much,' she said, 'I'll have to be going, soon.'

Half an hour later, she saw the time on the dash clock, and using that four-letter word of hers, pulled down her skirt and said she really must go. He drove back to the road, and she got into the Jag. He said he would reach her again after the trial, and waited to see how she would reply. Her face was enigmatic.

'All right,' she said.

He watched the white Jag disappear round a curve in the road, and then he walked slowly back to his car, sick to the stomach with black depression and bitter hatred.

It was only when he got back to his hotel in Castlebay that he remembered he had intended looking up Davies. He didn't think it would mean anything, but he went to find him.

2.

Next morning, after breakfast, Harry Deveen had the idea that he would like to visit Mrs. Merrill's grave in Castlebay churchyard.

He told Royston, and though Royston thought it was a morbid idea, and would have preferred to have browsed through the Sunday newspapers, he drove over to Castlebay with him.

Royston waited while Deveen went into the church-yard and disappeared in the direction of the grave.

He returned in a few moments looking white and it took him quite some time before he could tell Royston what had happened while he stood at the graveside.

The graveyard had appeared empty and silent, but as he approached Mrs. Merrill's grave a mongrel dog suddenly appeared, stood on the grave and snarled at him. Deveen spoke to it in a friendly way, but the mongrel would have gone for him, and he had to come away. He and Royston inquired at the church if the dog had been seen there before. Nobody knew of such a dog. People went to look, but there was no sign of the mongrel.

That night in the Bar Mess Royston was with Harry Deveen when the other put down his brandy to say to Ainger: 'I want, if I can, to get back to town by midweek. I've a case coming into the list next week.'

'We shan't finish until Wednesday, that's clear.'

'You have practically finished,' Deveen said.

'But you are calling Merrill, and there are the speeches and the summing-up; Lane doesn't like sitting after five, and I don't blame him.'

'It looks as if it'll go into the middle of the week; you'll be some time cross-examining Merrill.'

'Depends on what sort of a witness he is.'

'I think he'll put up a good show,'

Deveen said. 'The jury may want to take some time; I've been trying to size them up. I really can't make anything of them at all.'

'They may really be waiting for the summing-up; this is not an easy case, after all. Lane seems to have an open mind; he'll give your client a good run.'

A waiter came in and whispered in Claud Smithson's ear. Smithson followed him out. A few minutes later Smithson came back and spoke to Wells, and then went out of the room again. Wells came over to Ainger and Royston heard him say: 'Smithson would like to have a word with you. He says it's something important.'

Ainger got up and went to the door.

'What's the matter?' he said to Smithson who was waiting outside in the passage.

'Can I see you for a moment?'

Ainger nodded and went out of the room, closing the door behind him.

'Wonder what's up now?' Harry Deveen said to Wells, who gave him a noncommittal grin and walked across to the bookcase as if to read the titles of the books there. His manner was too obviously casual. Deveen looked across at Royston and they both sensed something in the atmosphere. And then Ainger came back into the room. He came straight over to Harry Deveen and Royston.

'Bit of a new development,' he said. 'The clerk, William Llewellyn, who used to be with your client, has turned up. Made a statement to the police about your client having arsenic in his possession. I don't know the details.'

Deveen got to his feet and glanced at Ainger uneasily.

'It's too late now,' he said, 'you've closed your case.'

'Yes, that's true. But if the effect of this statement is what I feel it might be, I shall certainly ask permission to call Llewellyn as a witness.'

Deveen scratched his chin. 'You have not given any notice of intention to call any additional witness,' he said; his tone was frank. 'I shall object to any fresh evidence being sprung upon us at the last moment.'

'It will hardly be sprung on you,' Ainger retorted, 'I've asked Smithson to let me have a copy of any statement made by Llewellyn, and his clerk's typing it out now. When I've seen it, he will let your solicitor have a copy, and give him notice of intention to call this additional witness. Sorry, but there it is.'

Harry Deveen said nothing, and sat down again; Smithson came in with some typewritten sheets in his hand, which he gave to Ainger, Wells, Deveen, and Royston. The latter two went to Deveen's room to talk over this sudden threat to Merrill. Royston thought Deveen looked a bit pale; and then suddenly he turned to him.

'I feel pretty rotten,' Deveen said.

'Excitement caused by this new twist,' Royston said.

'No, it's not that.'

'Chicken curry you had for dinner. You had a lot of it.'

'I feel a bit faint.' Deveen closed his eyes.

Royston helped him on to the bed, then hurried off and found Dr. Mortlake who was in his bedroom, and who put on a dressing-gown and went along to Deveen's room. 'Nothing seriously wrong,' he said to Deveen, after a few moments' examination, 'severe attack of indigestion. I've got some bismuth tablets; they'll soon put you right.'

Deveen groaned, and said to Mortlake: 'Don't confuse the tablets with anything else—arsenic, for example.'

Mortlake was back in a couple of minutes, and it was not long before Deveen reported that he felt much better.

'Too much chicken curry,' Royston said. 'I thought you overdid it.'

But Deveen had almost forgotten his indigestion attack; what he didn't feel so good about now was the idea of this new witness.

CHAPTER SEVENTEEN

Mr. Justice Lane took his seat the next morning, Monday 22nd October and Ainger asked for leave to call an additional witness.

'It is rather late, Mr. Attorney, is it not?'

'Yes, my lord, it is. May the jury retire while I explain the circumstances?'

The judge muttered something, and the jury filed out of court, their faces showing their speculation. Ainger handed the judge a copy of Llewellyn's statement.

On the day when Stone called at Merrill's office Llewellyn said that he had actually seen a packet labelled poison on Merrill's desk. He explained his failure to come forward before, by saying that a week later he had left Merrill's employment and had gone to live with a sister in a village near Armagh in Northern Ireland.

He had no knowledge of the Merrill case until an acquaintance from Castlebay visiting Armagh had chanced to meet him yesterday, and told him about the trial. 'I realized,' Llewellyn said, 'that my evidence might be important, and so I decided to take an airplane from Belfast that same evening. I arrived at

Manchester at eight p.m. and was driven straight to Castlebay, where I went to the police.'

'What do you say about this?' Mr. Justice Lane said to Deveen.

'My lord, I could say a lot about it; but I will confine myself to asking your lordship not to admit it. I never heard of this evidence until last night and the defence would be greatly prejudiced if your lordship were to accede to my learned friend's application. We have been taken completely by surprise. My client's solicitor has had no opportunity of taking instructions from the accused.'

The judge pulled at his long nose, and then decided that the best course would be for the Court to adjourn for half an hour, which would give Deveen and Royston an opportunity to see Merrill and take his further instructions.

Mr. Justice Lane went slowly from the court to his room, leaving behind him a buzz of conversation.

Merrill had gone down from the dock, and a prison officer opened the door leading from the court into the dock and Harry Deveen and Royston followed him down the short flight of stairs.

At the foot of the stairs there was an iron gate. It was locked. The prison officer pressed the bell alongside it and another prison officer appeared. He had a bunch of keys, and he opened the gate.

'We want to see Merrill for a few minutes,' Royston told him.

Merrill was not in a cell. He was in a musty, ill-lit

room with the senior prison officer who discreetly retired as Deveen and Royston came in.

'Of course, I want to shut out the statement from Llewellyn,' Deveen said at once. 'But I don't see how it can be done. Do you know of anything?'

'I know that Llewellyn's a damned liar,' Dick Merrill said.

'That won't help,' Deveen said quietly.

'I never had any packet of poison, so he must be a liar.'

'Not necessarily,' Deveen said. 'He may have been mistaken.'

'Not maybe,' Merrill said emphatically, 'must be mistaken. I never had any arsenic, I tell you.'

'I know what you said,' Deveen said. 'You'll have every opportunity of saying that when you go into the witness box.'

'Do your best to stop the evidence, and then I won't have to say what I'll have to say about that lying old bastard. It's not fair to spring it on us at the eleventh hour.'

Half an hour later the judge was back and Harry Deveen got to his feet. 'My lord, I have seen my client with his solicitor; and I am instructed to persist in my objection to the admissibility of this additional evidence.'

'Would you like an adjournment?'

'No, my lord, I do not think that is necessary.'

'Very good, Mr. Deveen, I understand your position, and I do not want you to feel embarrassed in any way.

But I feel that in the circumstances I ought to admit the additional evidence.'

Harry Deveen had no more to say, and he glanced at the dock where Merrill had followed all these discussions with evident anxiety. Now he watched intently as William Llewellyn made his way into the witness box. He was a grey-haired figure, short and fragile.

'Is your name William Llewellyn?' It was Ainger who took him through his examination-in-chief.

'It is.'

'What is your occupation, Mr. Llewellyn?'

'I haven't any now. I am retired, you know. I used to be with Mr. Merrill as his clerk.'

'And when did you give up your work?'

'Oh, a few months ago.'

'And what did you do then?'

'I went to a village near Armagh, in Northern Ireland on a visit to my sister. Soon after I arrived in Ireland she was taken very ill and I stayed on to look after her. Then I heard yesterday about this.'

'What did you hear?'

'Why, this about Mr. Merrill poisoning his wife and Mr. Stone with arsenic.'

'And when you heard this what did you do?'

'I felt I ought to come here and tell the judge what I know.'

'And is that how you came to be giving evidence now?'

'It is.'

'My lord,' said Ainger, 'may the witness see Mr.

Stone?'

Stone, who had been outside, came into court and stood there. 'Do you know that man?' Ainger turned to the figure in the witness box.

'Yes, I remember seeing him once.'

'Do you remember his name?'

'No, I can't say that I do,' and Llewellyn gave Stone an apologetic smile.

'Where did you see him?'

'At Mr. Merrill's office.'

'Do you remember the circumstances in which he came there?'

'Yes, I remember them very well. Somebody rang up and said he wanted to see Mr. Merrill.'

'Did he give his name?'

'Yes, he did.'

'Do you remember what it was?'

'No, I'm afraid I don't.'

'Do you remember what was said?'

Harry Deveen was up on his feet. 'My lord,' he said. 'Must we have what took place between this witness and some unknown stranger?'

It was a neat job of implication. Ainger said he wouldn't pursue the conversation.

'Let us come at once to the point,' he said to Llewellyn. 'Did you see this man come to the office?'

'Yes, very soon afterwards, he came to Mr. Merrill.' He nodded to Stone, who still stood there.

'We may take it that it was Mr. Stone.' Stone sat down in the well of the court. 'What happened next?'

'He said he wanted to see Mr. Merrill urgently,' Llewellyn said. 'I went in and told him.'

'Where was Merrill then?'

'He was sitting at his desk. I said a gentleman wanted to see him urgently. I must have given a name. I remember telling him that the gentleman seemed very angry.'

'What did the accused say?'

'I remember that very well; he said: 'Angry is he? I'll very soon make him quiet'.'

'And what did you do?'

'I went out and I told him,' he nodded in Stone's direction, 'that Mr. Merrill would see him and I showed him in.'

'Now, Mr. Llewellyn, did anything attract your attention?'

'Yes, sir.'

'What was it?'

'When I showed him into the office I saw something on Mr. Merrill's desk, a white package open one end, it was. I caught a glimpse of the label, and I distinctly saw it said poison in red at the top and something written underneath, but I couldn't see what it was. There were some words at the bottom of the label, also in red. But I couldn't see what they were.'

'Did you see the accused do anything?'

'Yes, I saw him quickly open a drawer in his desk and put the package in.'

'And did you leave the accused and Mr. Stone together?'

'Yes, I did.'

'What was the next thing that happened?'

'Mr. Merrill came out and asked me to make them some tea. Two cups, he told me, one for himself and one for the other one. I used to make tea for him in the office, and sometimes a caller.'

'And did you make tea?'

'Yes.'

'And took in two cups?'

'Yes.'

'And how long did Mr. Stone stay?'

'Not very long.'

'And did you go into the inner office?'

'Yes, I did. I saw that one of the cups was empty and the other was still full.'

'And did the accused say anything?'

'Yes, he said his visitor didn't want tea, after all.'

'Do you remember anything else?'

'No, I think that is all.'

Ainger sat down and now Harry Deveen got up on his feet to cross-examine.

'Do you really mean to say,' he said, without looking at the witness box, but keeping his eyes on the jury, 'that you heard nothing about this case until yesterday?'

'That's quite true.'

'Although the newspapers have been full of the case?'

'I never saw an English paper while I was away.'

'That may be so, but surely the Irish papers had something about it?'

'They may have done, but I didn't see anything.'

'So it must have come as a shock to you to learn of your one-time employer being on trial for murder?'

'Yes.'

'And you decided there and then to rush here and give evidence against him?'

'Well, I remembered what I have just said about the package on his desk.'

'When you say you remembered are you sure that is the right word?'

'Well, yes. It came back to me.'

'Or do you think you may have imagined it?'

'Imagined it?' Llewellyn said, with evident surprise.

'Yes, imagined it.' Now Deveen turned upon him, and his face appeared more shark-like than ever. 'If Merrill says he had never had poison in his possession, either on his desk or anywhere else, do you not think you may have been mistaken?'

Llewellyn hesitated momentarily. He turned to the judge. 'I am quite clear what I saw,' he said firmly. 'Otherwise I wouldn't have come all this way to tell you about it.'

'And you are quite clear,' Deveen said, 'in your recollection of what was said?'

Llewellyn turned back to Deveen. 'Yes,' he said.

'Did the accused say: 'I'll very soon quieten him down'?'

'I thought he said: 'I'll very soon make him quiet.' He may have said what you suggest.'

'And it was a very natural thing to say?'

'I thought so at the time.'

'When did you change your mind?'

'When I heard all this about the arsenic.'

'When you discovered that your employer was charged with murder?'

'Yes, that's correct.'

Harry Deveen stared at him, then with a shrug at the jury as much as to say he regretted wasting their time, he sat down.

CHAPTER EIGHTEEN

1.

Philip Vane had slipped in at the back of the court to see Llewellyn in the witness box and to try and judge what impact his evidence would have. As he watched that wispy little man blinking at Harry Deveen he felt sure that he had put the noose around Dick Merrill's neck.

No less than that, he felt.

As Ainger now stood up, Vane knew why Deveen had been much too smart to try and put into the jury's mind that Llewellyn had come forward out of spite for some wrong, real or imagined, which he had suffered at Merrill's hands.

'Mr. Llewellyn,' Ainger was saying, 'why have you taken the trouble to come here and tell us what you know about someone in whose employ you had been, who had been kind and considerate to you?'

Llewellyn's eyes shifted from Ainger to the blond, suntanned figure in the dock, then back to Ainger.

'I just thought it was right that the truth should be told about poor Mr. Stone's illness,' he said.

Ainger turned to the judge. 'My lord, that is the case

for the Crown.'

Before Llewellyn had shown up, Vane's estimate was that Deveen was calculating on Merrill's evidence and the impression he gave in the witness box, that was going to prove the acid test. Merrill could win his life for himself.

Looking at the jury, it was that sort of jury; they wouldn't convict if Merrill gave them half a chance not to. That was until Llewellyn's surprise appearance had loaded the dice. Harry Deveen was getting slowly to his feet.

'My lord I call the accused.'

Vane had caught a glimpse of Margot Stone from where he stood; he felt sure she had not seen him. He saw her profile as Deveen called Dick Merrill and only her eyes had widened a little, that was all. He couldn't tell if Merrill looked at her; probably not, it wouldn't help him with the jury.

There was silence, only the scrape of Merrill's chair in the dock as he got up and followed by a prison officer, made his way to the witness box.

Harry Deveen's examination-in-chief took him along to create a picture of a popular, happily married type, settling down to a prosperous business career. Now, Deveen came to the heart of it.

'Have you ever had any poison of any kind in your possession?'

'Poison? Never in my life. Why should I want poison?'

'You have only to answer questions. You say you

have never had any poison in your possession. Did your wife possess any?'

'My wife, as I said in my statement to the police, bought some arsenic for killing weeds. But I had nothing to do with that.'

'Do you know what became of it?'

'As far as I know it was used by her, and if any remained it was thrown away. I certainly never had any.'

'Your wife apparently died from arsenical poisoning. Can you throw any light on that?'

'No; it's a mystery to me. Of course, she was very depressed at times. Whether she took any intentionally or by accident, I do not know. I'd always assumed she died from natural causes.'

'Did you get on well with your wife?'

'Yes, I was very fond of her.'

'You had no reason for wanting to get rid of her?'

'None.'

'Had you any particular affection for Mrs. Stone?'

'I liked her, and still like her. But there has never been anything between us. Just a harmless flirtation, that's all.'

'The witness, Gwladys Williams, said that Mrs. Stone came to your house after your wife's death? What do you say about that?'

'It is untrue. Mrs. Stone may have visited Fancy during my wife's lifetime, but certainly not after her death. I think that is where the mistake arose in Mrs. Stone's statement.'

But Deveen brushed that aside. 'And had you any reason to get rid of Mr. Stone?'

'Certainly not.'

'You may remember Mr. Stone came to see you at your office, by himself?'

'Yes, I remember that.'

'Did you have any poison, any arsenic, for instance, in your possession at that time?'

'Of course I did not.'

'You heard what the witness, Llewellyn, said about seeing a package on your desk?'

'That is absolute nonsense. I know nothing about it.'

'Do you remember asking for two cups of tea?'

'I may have done, I can't remember.'

'At the dinner party, when Mr. and Mrs. Stone came to your house, did you have any arsenic in your possession then?'

'I tell you I have never had any arsenic in my possession, then or at any other time.' Merrill raised his voice. 'I don't invite people to dinner and then try to poison them.'

'The suggestion is that you attempted to poison Mr. Stone.'

'That is untrue. I am completely innocent.'

Deveen gave him a faint encouraging smile, and then he sat down. Ainger was on his feet, slipping his pince-nez off and on and wading into the attack.

'Take in your hand Exhibit 6,' he said, sharp-toned. 'The statement you made to the police.' Merrill took the statement, it didn't shake in his hand. He had his nerves well under control. 'You see where you wrote: 'I remember how the lawn at the back became infested with weeds, and my impression is that my wife purchased some arsenic to kill them. I think I may have suggested that she should get some arsenic from a local chemist for use in killing weeds. I am almost sure it was Ivor Pryce'?'

'Yes, I see that.'

'Would I be wrong to say that you meant to obtain that arsenic, but preferred that it should be bought by your wife and not by you?'

'You would be utterly wrong.'

'If arsenic was needed for killing weeds, why did you not get it?'

'Because my wife looked after the garden.'

'And you don't know whether she used all the arsenic or not?'

'No, I do not.'

'So some of it may have been left over?'

'It may have been, but I don't think so.'

'You do not know?'

'Not for certain.'

'If any was left over it could have been in your possession?'

'It could have been, but it never was.'

'It is remarkable is it not, that Mr. Llewellyn says he saw a package on your desk labelled poison?'

'It is more than remarkable, it's absolutely fantastic.'

'The suggestion made by my learned friend, as I understand it, was that Mr. Llewellyn must have been imagining it?'

'I can't think of any other explanation.'

'So Mr. Llewellyn is mistaken?'

'People do make mistakes sometimes.'

Merrill glared round the courtroom as if to say that it was a mistake that he was there at all.

Ainger went on to question him closely if Llewellyn had been in the habit of making mistakes while in his employ; Merrill dealt with this line quite neatly, making the point that his clerk could have made mistakes which he had covered up, and Merrill also worked in the obvious fact of Llewellyn's age which need not be conducive to clear-mindedness or good memory. Ainger got back to the poison package.

'He says he saw a package on your desk, labelled poison. You cannot suggest any explanation of Llewellyn's mistake over this, if it was a mistake?'

'I can't, but he certainly was mistaken.'

'You heard Gwladys Williams say that she saw Mrs. Stone at your house after your wife's death?'

'Mrs. Stone never came to my house after my wife died.'

'And you heard the same witness say she overheard you say to Mrs. Stone: 'Why don't you leave him'?'

'All absolute rubbish.'

'And, according to Gwladys Williams, Mrs. Stone said to you: 'I can't do that, Dick, much as I love you'.'

'Mrs. Stone does not love me, any more than I love her. We like each other, that's all. And I did flirt with her, it's true.'

'Then Gwladys Williams must have invented everything that she said in the witness box?'

'She must have done.'

'She was on oath; why should she invent a thing like that?'

'Why don't you ask Gwladys Williams.'

'I'm asking you.'

'And I'm telling you I don't know, except that perhaps she felt vindictive towards me over something. Some women do get funny ideas about things.'

'You don't know what funny ideas she got about you?'

'I'm afraid I don't.'

'So it comes to this, Merrill: your ex-clerk, Llewellyn, is mistaken in what he said in his evidence?'

'Yes.'

'And Gwladys Williams is mistaken?'

'Yes.'

'But you can't think why they should be so mistaken?'

'No, I can't.'

'And the experts at Cardiff police laboratory, are they mistaken too?'

'You mean about the arsenic in the urine?'

'If you did not have arsenic in your possession at any time, is it not rather remarkable that within a short time of dining at your house Mr. Stone should have been taken suddenly ill with arsenical poisoning?'

'It had nothing to do with me.'

'Let me ask you this: did you love your wife?'

'I was very fond of her, we were very good friends,

we had complete trust and faith in each other. But I didn't love her, no. She realized that. I have admitted all this.'

'Finally, then, let me ask you this. Did you love Mrs. Stone?'

'I like her.'

'I asked you whether you loved her?'

'I have told you that I flirted with her, but I didn't love her. After all, she was another man's wife.'

Ainger stood staring at Merrill for a moment or two and then he sat down.

Deveen got up again, and had only one question to put in re-examination. It was the standard one. 'Merrill, did you murder your wife?'

'I certainly did not.'

'Thank you.'

The judge had one question.

'Merrill, when Mr. Llewellyn left your employment, was there any unpleasantness between you?'

'No, my lord, none whatever.'

Looking pale and his mouth thin, his pale blue eyes a little glazed-looking, Merrill took his seat again in the dock between the two prison officers. He had been in the witness box nearly an hour and a half.

Vane didn't like the look of it, but he could be wrong.

He could leave the rest of it to Davies, as usual. He had to get back to London.

2.

The only other evidence for the defence that Deveen could call was medical evidence to refute Mortlake and Wiltshire; and next into the witness box was Dr. Soutar, who described himself as an advisory medical officer of various insurance companies, constantly engaged in investigating cases of accidents and industrial diseases. He had done over seven thousand P.M.'s, he said.

'I have seen one fatal case of acute poisoning,' he said, 'one case of acute poisoning which recovered, and I have seen several cases of sub-acute poisoning, and also of chronic poisoning. I have seen many cases of poisoning from other causes.' The course of Mrs. Merrill's illness, he said, and the post-mortem, indicated that in all probability her death was caused by arsenic taken about 16th January 1956, but none before. 'It must have been a large dose.'

In reply to the judge who asked him what he meant by a large dose, Dr. Soutar said: 'I should call seven or six grains a large dose. I think more than six grains must have been taken in this case, because of the amount found after death. But it is difficult to assess the precise amount, because vomiting upsets the whole calculations.'

'Supposing,' Harry Deveen said, 'Mrs. Merrill had taken a large dose on 16th January, what, in view of her symptoms, in your opinion happened?'

'It seems to me that a large portion of the arsenic became encapsuled, that is to say caught up in a fold of the stomach lining. I myself have had experience of a case when a patient took a large dose of arsenic, and yet lived seven days. The post-mortem revealed that the arsenic had become encapsuled in the patient's stomach.'

'Supposing that this large dose was given on the 16th January, would that in your opinion account for what was found at the post-mortem?'

'Quite.'

'Would it also account for the symptoms which were shown during Mrs. Merrill's last illness?'

'Yes.'

Deveen turned to Stone's illness. Dr. Soutar considered that his symptoms were consistent either with an attack of acute indigestion or gastrointestinal influenza, or an irritant poison, which would include arsenic.

'There is a symptom which is decidedly against it having been arsenic,' he said. 'That is the fact that Mr. Stone was fully recovered, I think, in four or five days. If he had taken a fatal dose of arsenic he would be unlikely to feel so well after so short an interval; I think it would take at least a fortnight.'

Harry Deveen next dealt with the manner in which Dr. Griffiths had obtained the urine sample.

'I should say that it was not taken in a scientific way at all,' Dr. Soutar said. 'The bottle previously contained peroxide of hydrogen, which ordinary washing would not necessarily remove.'

Cross-examining Dr. Soutar, Ainger came to Mrs. Merrill's peripheral neuritis symptoms. 'The high-stepping walk which Dr. Griffiths described, is that not a symptom of peripheral neuritis brought about by arsenical poisoning?'

'It is a symptom, yes, but it is not confined to arsenical poisoning; other things would cause the high-stepping walk.'

'I am not talking about the other things. I am confining myself to a case where you have peripheral neuritis caused by arsenical poisoning. In such a case is not the high-stepping walk characteristic?'

Dr. Soutar agreed that it was; and then he was re-examined by Harry Deveen.

'Now Dr. Soutar, putting it quite straight, do cases of arsenic becoming encapsuled in the stomach take place?'

'They do.'

'And if they take place, do you then get the arsenic gradually becoming dispersed through the stomach?'

'Yes, you would find that the arsenic had dispersed through the intestine, which is what occurred in this case.'

It was the end of Dr. Soutar's evidence and the court adjourned until next day.

CHAPTER NINETEEN

Next morning, Tuesday, 23rd October, Harry Deveen put Julian York, F.R.C.S., practising in Liverpool, in the witness box. He, too, felt perfectly certain that Mrs. Merrill had died of a large dose of arsenic which was taken about 16th January or 17th January.

'Would you say,' Deveen said, 'that in your opinion this dose of arsenic was the first she ever had?'

'That would be my opinion, yes.'

'And the last and only dose?'

'Yes,' York said. It was quite consistent with the symptoms during Mrs. Merrill's illness, and what was found at the post-mortem. York came to the evidence with regard to Stone. 'I do not think the proper methods were used to take a test in a serious matter like this. Had I been testing for poison, I should have washed out the bottle a few times with boiling water, so to have a better chance of dissolving any arsenic there; and sent the last washing to the analyst with the sample bottle as well.'

'Do you regard yourself as a competent judge in a case of arsenical poisoning, which is a matter for common sense as well as highly specialized knowledge?' And Deveen threw one of his glances at the jury.

York agreed; he had the symptoms to go by and the results of the post-mortem. Mrs. Merrill had died of arsenical poisoning, but if she had taken arsenic on 16th January she must have had a dose half an hour to an hour before becoming ill. That was common sense, he said, based on his knowledge of the action of arsenic. He went on to say that though, in his experience, he had never come across a case of encapsuled poison, he had seen it mentioned in case histories.

'Do you think,' Harry Deveen said, 'the symptoms from which Mrs. Merrill suffered before that time were consistent with arsenical poisoning, for instance, the high-stepping walk?'

'A high-stepping walk is not necessarily consistent with arsenical poisoning. It could be a symptom of a great many other things. Vomiting is a symptom I should expect from arsenical poisoning, but it does not always occur.'

Ainger now got up to cross-examine.

'In the case of Mr. Stone,' he said, 'does this history of one thirty-third of a grain in his urine indicate nothing to you?'

'If I were absolutely certain that he had passed that urine with that quantity of arsenic in it, then obviously he must have taken some arsenic to have given him that amount.'

'That would be a matter of common sense,' Ainger agreed humourlessly, careful not to give the impression that he was enjoying a little quiet sarcasm at the other's expense. 'Supposing after four days he passed one thirty-third of a grain, what do you think he would have taken four days previously?'

'We have absolutely no data upon which we can offer any opinion.'

'Are you familiar with a paper written by Sir Martin Wiltshire in 1947 which was a particular study of traces of arsenic being found in urine some days after having been administered?'

'I know that Sir Martin has made a number of tests.'

'What is your experience of arsenical poisoning cases?'

'As a matter of fact, I have had no cases of acute arsenical poisoning in my experience.'

'May I take it that you say that Sir Martin Wiltshire's evidence as to the amount of arsenic found in the urine after the administration of arsenic is all incorrect?'

'I have not said so; but I do say this most emphatically that we have no knowledge of the way he carried out his tests. Different methods might yield different results in certain aspects.'

'Do you or do you not agree that Sir Martin is the greatest authority on arsenical poisoning?'

'In this country I would say he is.'

'We are dealing with a case which has occurred in this country,' Ainger said, and he sat down.

Julian York patted his face with his handkerchief and left the witness box.

Harry Deveen began his closing speech by reminding

the jury that they were trying Merrill on a charge of having murdered his wife; they were not trying him on a charge of attempting to murder Stone. The evidence in Stone's case was dragged in, he said, simply to bolster up the prosecution's case against Merrill.

Nearly always at any murder trial the accused seems to add an air of dignity to his own personality; while all the wrangling is going on about him, he alone sits there quietly, taking it all, the good and the bad that is being said about him. Merrill was no exception; there was a feeling of guts about him that could not fail to gain him sympathy.

'What sort of case is this, then, that has been brought against him,' Deveen was saying, 'that the prosecution must prop it up with this idea that because he did the one he must have done the other, and vice versa? But Mrs. Merrill's death is what counts here; and what was the cause for suspicion? It was not until Stone was found to be suffering from arsenical poisoning that Dr. Griffiths became suspicious, previously he had given the death certificate for something quite different.'

Dealing with the lack of proof that Merrill had ever bought any arsenic, although the police had made the most exhaustive inquiries in the hope, as Deveen put it, of discovering that he had, he sniped at Llewellyn's last-minute evidence. Was it believable that this man could come forward and honestly say that he had never heard of this case until a day or two ago?

'He has been, so he says, in Northern Ireland, looking after a sick sister. Did that take up so much of his time that he had none left to read the newspapers?'

The Irish newspapers would be making this case front-page news. If the jury thought it may have escaped his notice, of what weight was his evidence? 'An elderly man who does not see glaring newspaper reports of a murder case which features the familiar names of his late employer or his hometown, can you believe that his mind is so sharp that he can reliably recall some incident which occurred several months ago?'

Merrill had strongly denied that he ever had any arsenic in his possession, so this last-minute witness, Deveen said, was produced like a trump card out of a clear blue sky, though he didn't even know Stone's name, to say that his one-time employer is a liar.

'Who is right, Llewellyn or Merrill, on trial before you for his very life? If he was, in fact, in possession of arsenic, can you imagine for one moment imagine him being so stupid as to display it on his desk, where it could be seen by Llewellyn or anyone else?'

Could the jury honestly believe, he added, that a man poisoning his wife, would go out of his way to call in his own doctor, the very person who was most likely to find him out?

'Dr. Griffiths, who was attending Mrs. Merrill all that time, never once suspected that she was being given arsenic by anyone, let alone her devoted husband. Of course, Mrs. Merrill did not die a natural death. Dr. Griffiths admits, with admirable honesty, he was wrong about that. And no blame attaches to him, we all make mistakes. Even the most expert doctors.'

Deveen paused to let his gaze flicker over Mortlake and the other medical witnesses for the prosecution. He came to Nurse Howells's evidence.

'She said that from 16th January up to the date of her death Mrs. Merrill never got out of bed. But Nurse Howells was not with her patient every moment of the night and day; that would be impossible for even a devoted nurse like Nurse Howells. Are you going to say that Mrs. Merrill could not have found a moment in which she could have taken the poison herself? It is not for me to prove that she did or did not; but if she did, the doctors I have called say that her symptoms up to her death were consistent with her taking one large dose on or about 16th January, five days before she died, symptoms consistent with suicide, and not with murder.'

When the Attorney-General was opening his case, Deveen went on, he had asked who could have done this murder, who had a motive for doing it, and he had pointed to Merrill.

'I could answer that Mrs. Merrill could have done it herself. Who could have been in possession of arsenic for the purpose of doing it? Mrs. Merrill. What was her motive? Who can say what a woman may be thinking? She may have discovered her husband's flirtation with Mrs. Stone, and she may have allowed it to prey on her mind. She may have had other secret reasons why she could not face living. Suicides do not tell their secret fears, even to their dearest friends.'

He came to Stone, and here again, he said, there was nothing to prove that he had suffered from arsenical poisoning, except the analysis showing one thirty-third of a grain in his urine. The doctors for the prosecution as well as the defence agreed that his symptoms were not like Mrs. Merrill's; they were more consistent with gastric enteritis or gastric influenza. There were several ways in which he could have absorbed arsenic, without Merrill giving it him.

He turned to Merrill's own evidence. 'He went into the witness box though he need not have done so. It was open to him quite rightly to have said, as many a man does, faced with a criminal charge: "I am innocent, and it is up to you to prove your case against me. I am quite content to remain where I am and to rely on the statement which I have made." But Merrill is one of your neighbours, a businessman working in your midst; he wants to stay that way, for you to believe him and tell the world that you believe that he is an innocent man; he wants you to let him walk among you again, his head held high, and free.'

Merrill's story in the witness box was the story that he had always told. Probed by question after question, tested as no man has ever been tested before, Deveen said, was there any difference anywhere in his evidence?

'Was not his evidence, in the beginning, in the middle and at the end, what you would expect from someone honest and unafraid?'

Harry Deveen was building up to his climax; he was

talking to the jury now as he might be giving some man-to-man advice to an old friend.

'When the Attorney-General was cross-examining Merrill it was not on the spur of the moment; it was the result of a great deal of anxious thought and study. And Merrill answered every question frankly and truthfully. Members of the jury, the time is very near when you must ask yourselves a question. Is Merrill proved guilty up to the hilt, beyond any reasonable doubt? You must each of you give your answer as he gave his, honestly and truthfully. You cannot afford to make a mistake, for on your answer Richard Merrill's life—or death—depends.'

CHAPTER TWENTY

Deveen's closing speech had taken him to the end of the day; and Mr. Justice Lane adjourned until the next day, while the jury went off to the hotel at the other end of Caernarvon where all twelve of them were staying.

The next morning, Wednesday, 24th October, when they returned to their place in the jury box, Ainger got to his feet slowly, removing his pince-nez and replacing it upon his nose and told the jury plainly that the burden of proof in this case rested on the Crown.

It was for the Crown to satisfy them beyond reasonable doubt of the guilt of the accused, if guilt there be.

By its frankness and its fair-mindedness Ainger's whole tone began to enlist the jury's interest and growing understanding. When he had decided they were ready for it, Ainger struck.

'Now, members of the jury, you may well think that this whole case hinges upon the evidence of William Llewellyn. If you accept his evidence, then it is clear beyond the possibility of argument that the accused was in possession of poison at the time when Stone called upon him at his office. If he was, then you will have little doubt that he was in possession of it at the time of the dinner party, and that he attempted to poison Mr. Stone.'

He paused as if awaiting their unspoken agreement to his argument.

'But the evidence goes further than that,' he went on, conveying the impression that, of course, they did agree with him. 'If the accused attempted to poison Mr. Stone, the poison he used was arsenic. What was he doing, secretly using a lethal poison, and denying that he had it, unless it was for some deadly and surreptitious purpose? It was not aspirin he was hiding, or soda mints, it was this murderous arsenic. If then he used arsenic to poison Stone, have you any doubt that he had it secretly during his wife's illness, and that she died from arsenical poisoning?'

If they accepted this, he said, then they must be left in no doubt as to the accused's guilt.

'Now, members of the jury,' and Ainger's voice became more urgent in its appeal, 'I doubt whether poison is ever witnessed being administered. You are able to act on evidence sure and certain in other cases, but in a case of poisoning you will always find subtlety and cunning attempts to cover up the tracks of so inscrutable a crime.'

The defence admitted that Mrs. Merrill died of arsenic. 'How was that poison administered to her? "Suicide," says my learned friend; and he also suggested that Mrs. Merrill's symptoms were due to acute indigestion and rheumatism, causing toxaemia, which in turn caused peripheral neuritis which produced the symptoms confused with arsenical poisoning.'

And, Ainger added, because of the great experience and ability of Dr. Mortlake, Wiltshire and Kilrain, their evidence ought to be discounted in favour of the prisoner. But surely in investigating this case of the death of a subject of the Crown, the Crown is obliged to engage experts of the highest ability?

According to their evidence, Ainger went on, arsenical poisoning has an immediate effect on the stomach. First, vomiting; secondly, after the vomiting and the arsenic itself has been expelled, upon the nervous system, causing peripheral neuritis; not local neuritis in one joint, but in the nerves and extremities of the limbs generally.

'Mrs. Merrill showed all of those symptoms quite clearly. Were these symptoms due to arsenical poisoning, or to toxaemia? I ask you to accept Dr. Griffiths's evidence and that of the others that she was suffering from arsenical poisoning. On 11th January Dr. Griffiths called, and he endeavoured to get Mrs. Merrill to walk. He described how she complained of this high-stepping walk, a symptom of peripheral neuritis, which can be caused by toxaemia—or arsenical poisoning.'

During the last four days of her life Mrs. Merrill was lying helpless, unable to take any food, according to her trusted physician, observing her day by day.

He dealt with the possibility of suicide; that because the arsenic she had herself taken became encapsuled in her stomach with consequent delayed action, she did not die until four days later. 'No word was revealed by her that she contemplated poisoning herself. Can you believe it?'

Ainger paused and let his gaze range over the faces before him, then resumed his button-holing technique.

'Members of the jury, there is one certainty about this case, and it is that a doctor can tell, within a few hours, at what time an arsenic dose must have been taken; and all the doctors for the Crown have told you that there must have been a fatal dose administered to Mrs. Merrill within twenty-four hours of her death, and that the idea of suicide was an impossible one to believe.'

He turned to the question of motive.

'Not all the wealth of the Indies could offer you or me a motive for committing a crime so terrible as this murder. But some people might reckon £5,000 a suitable motive for murder, others might do it for £50,000. Or perhaps not money at all; perhaps Merrill did it because he was out of love with his own wife, and in love with someone else's.'

As for Stone, the jury should ask themselves whether the opportunity for poisoning Stone by arsenic arose and was taken at Merrill's dinner party. 'The defence say that this trace of arsenic in Stone's urine may have arisen from a dirty bottle. Mr. Pryce, a chemist of experience and repute, selected the bottle; he tells you he washed it half-a-dozen times, he realized the importance of a clean bottle.'

The fact was that Stone went home after having

dinner with Merrill, became ill, vomited throughout the night, suffered severe stomach pains and subsequently one thirty-third of a grain of arsenic was found in his urine.

'The extraordinary similarity between the symptoms in both Stone's illness and that of Mrs. Merrill is so remarkable that you have the confident opinion of the experts that they arose from the same cause, poisoning by arsenic. Who had the opportunity and the means to administer that arsenic? Who had the motive?'

Ainger began building to his climax.

'My learned friend has called your attention to the fact that this is a matter of life and death. Yes; but whose life? Whose death? Has there not arisen before you the scene at this house named Fancy, of that wretchedly sick wife lying there helpless, meeting an agonizing death? By whose hand? I say, by the prisoner's hand. If the evidence that you have heard compels you to agree that I am right, your duty is plain, and I therefore ask you to say that the prisoner is Guilty.'

It was about an hour after the court had resumed when Ainger finished his closing speech, and he sat down.

CHAPTER TWENTY-ONE

Philip Vane had driven up early that morning in time to be there for the summing-up. Royston was full of optimism.

'Deveen has done a wonderful job.'

Mr. Justice Lane explained to the jury that he would direct them as to the Law. What they had to concern themselves with, he said, were the facts of the case as they had been brought out in evidence. It was not for them to try anything else but this charge made against the prisoner that he had murdered his wife by poisoning her.

After underscoring that Merrill was entitled to the benefit of the doubt, the judge made it clear that it was all circumstantial evidence, that the jury had heard. No one had actually seen Merrill give his wife arsenic.

Philip Vane stood at the back of the musty little court; from where he was he couldn't see Margot Stone, as the judge went on: 'If you came across a dead man lying on a path it would be unreasonable of you to suppose that he had necessarily been killed by a poacher. But if you knew that the dead man was a gamekeeper who was always on the look-out for poachers, and you had arrived in time to see a notorious poacher running away from the body, then you would be in possession of sound circumstantial evidence for believing that the poacher had killed the gamekeeper.'

He was a good judge; Vane had heard him before, sometimes when he'd thought he hadn't been so good. That time when he'd sent Vane down was one of the times.

There was the question of opportunity, Mr. Justice Lane was saying. Obviously Merrill had the opportunity of poisoning his wife with arsenic. 'He was in the house with her; he was married to her.'

But even if they thought he had every possible opportunity to bring about his wife's death, they must not therefore jump to conclusions.

'The experts found in her body more arsenic than they, who are accustomed to deal with these things, have found in any exhumed body before. That being so, could it be that she took it accidentally? Or did she take it herself with intent to take her own life for reasons which, though they may be impossible for them to fathom, cannot necessarily be ruled out?'

As for motive, he echoed Ainger's argument, he advised the jury not to give much thought to it; the next point was Stone. 'It was submitted that his case had nothing to do with this one, where Merrill is charged with murdering his wife. I decided that the evidence respecting Stone was relevant here and that you should hear it.'

He sipped from the glass of water before him. 'If

you decide that Merrill did not give Stone arsenic with intent to kill him, then the evidence in that case has no bearing whatever on the case of Mrs. Merrill. But if you come to the conclusion that he did give it to Stone, then it shows that he had got poison and that he was prepared to put it to deadly use. And you might say that what he did to Stone, he had also done to his wife.'

He came to Mrs. Merrill's illness; how she had suffered from peripheral neuritis. 'According to the prosecution it was caused by arsenical poisoning. According to the defence it was caused by toxaemia.' He summarized the doctors' evidence; Dr. Mortlake, Sir Martin Wiltshire and Dr. Griffiths; Dr. Soutar and Julian York.

It was a matter of deciding which medical witness they believed; and he reviewed Mortlake's powerful evidence, his post-mortem on Mrs. Merrill had showed that a large dose was taken within twenty-four hours of her death, and other poisonous doses had been taken during the preceding four or five days. Wiltshire had also said that there must have been several doses taken from 16th January to 21st January; and that Mrs. Merrill had taken a large dose of arsenic within twenty-four hours of her death, and that she could not herself have taken it within the last four or five days.

'Mr. York, however, says death was caused by arsenic taken on 16th January and none after. It was a large dose of arsenic which in his view became encapsuled in the stomach. Could this dose of arsenic have become lodged in the stomach for several days before it acted? Dr. Soutar, also for the defence, but who had no experience of arsenical poisoning, said that Mrs. Merrill died as the result of a dose of arsenic taken on or about 16th January, which had become encapsuled and lain wait, so to speak, until 21st January.'

Mrs. Merrill had died from arsenical poisoning; arsenic had been available at Fancy, Merrill had said she had bought it.

'You may think it strange that he did not know that there was any arsenic in the house; or you may think he was lying, that he knew only too well it was there.'

Next, Llewellyn. 'The prosecution produced what they ask you to accept as a piece of direct evidence that Merrill was, in fact, in possession of poison at or about the time of Stone's illness. Was Llewellyn telling the truth when he described to you how, when Stone, who seemed angry, called at Merrill's office, the accused said: 'Angry is he? I'll very soon make him quiet'? And do you believe that just afterwards Llewellyn saw on Merrill's desk a white package, open at one end?'

The judge was referring to his notes, and then looking down his long nose at the jury. He read out. 'I distinctly saw it said poison in red at the top and something written underneath,' Llewellyn said, 'but I couldn't see what it was. There was some words at the bottom of the label, also in red. But I couldn't see what they were.' Llewellyn saw Merrill hurriedly put the package in his desk drawer. Very detailed evidence, and you have to ask yourselves whether it is possible that Llewellyn could have imagined the whole incident.'

Mr. Justice Lane pointed out that before Llewellyn's evidence it had been established that Merrill asked Llewellyn to make a cup of tea for Stone and one for himself. Llewellyn had recalled this clearly; had he been equally reliable when he said he said he saw the white package labelled poison on Merrill's desk?

'If what he says was true, then you may think Merrill intended to poison Stone's tea; and if that was his purpose, you may also believe that the poison was arsenic, which he had at the time of his wife's illness and with which he poisoned her to death.'

The shadows began to creep about the court, and the dusk lying in wait outside moved in, as the judge came to the end of it. 'Remember what you have heard about the burden of proof, that it is for the prosecution to establish their case. And now will you please consider your verdict, and say how you find, whether you find the accused Guilty or Not Guilty.'

CHAPTER TWENTY-TWO

1.

They were out for only twenty-three minutes. They came slowly back and made their way into their places in the jury box. Not one of them looked at the figure in the dock; Vane knew what that meant. The Clerk of the Assize cleared his throat. 'Members of the jury, are you agreed on your verdict?'

'We are,' the foreman said.

'Do you find the prisoner Richard Merrill Guilty or Not Guilty?'

'Guilty.'

Merrill went deathly pale behind that tan of his.

Vane shifted a little so that he could get a good look round the silent courtroom; it was as if everyone had stopped breathing. She wasn't there.

'Prisoner at the bar,' the Clerk of the Assize said, 'you stand convicted of murder. Have you anything to say why the court should not give you judgment according to law?'

'Only that I still say I am innocent.'

The black square of cloth slightly askew on his wig the judge, his voice a rasp, sentenced him to death.

In the cell beneath the court Vane joined Royston and Deveen, and found Merrill smiling. 'What are you looking so miserable for?' he was saying to Royston, and then he saw Vane. 'And if you've come for your confession,' he said, 'you're not getting it. Not yet.'

His pale-blue gaze seemed to see right inside Vane's skull. For a moment Vane experienced a terrible compulsion to spill everything. But he didn't, he just swallowed and put up a smile.

'We shall appeal, of course,' Deveen was saying briskly. 'Don't you worry, Merrill, they'll throw this out in London, that's for sure.'

Charlie Wraysbury and his assistant arrived at Strangeways Prison, Manchester, at four p.m. the day before the execution was due to take place; they wouldn't be allowed to leave until after nine o'clock the next morning.

Charlie Wraysbury was given all the information he needed about Dick Merrill's height and weight; and he had a look at him while he was exercising without himself being seen.

Working to the official table of the average length of drop required according to height and weight, added to what he had seen of him walking alone round the exercise-yard, Charlie Wraysbury was able to assess just what would suit Dick Merrill.

The execution shed outside the condemned cell was all ready, and while Merrill was still exercising Charlie Wraysbury and his assistant were able to test the working of the trap with a bag of sand the same weight as the man they had come to hang. They left the bag hanging overnight to stretch the rope.

It is important for the record to know how much the rope stretches; which is why after Charlie Wraysbury pulled the lever punctually at nine o'clock the next morning, Merrill was left swinging very slightly, for an hour before he was taken down and the prison works officer measured the rope to see how much it had stretched.

It had hardly stretched at all; Dick Merrill had lost a lot of weight in prison.

His only chance in an appeal to the Court of Criminal Appeal had been the point about the admissibility of the evidence in the case of Stone; and Harry Deveen had done his best. But the Lord Chief Justice referred to the Armstrong Case and the Geering Case; Merrill's case was covered by these earlier decisions.

If only he had waited a few months, they wouldn't have hanged him, anyway. The Homicide Bill, under which poisoners only got life, twelve years, in fact, came in the following March.

About two months after it was all forgotten, Philip Vane found himself once again in Castlebay.

He knew that the bungalow called Tamarisk was up for sale: Margot Stone had last been heard of somewhere in the South of France, Stone was living in London. And then the gossip and speculation had quickly died away, even in a small place like Castlebay plenty went on to occupy people's minds.

So he had driven up from London and put up at the

'Antelope.' After dinner he'd walked up Castlebay High Street, up the hill to Dr. Griffiths's house.

The Merrill business apparently hadn't touched him very much. He'd collected a few more patients who had come to him hoping to learn something extra about what had gone on at the Merrills; and there was a new trout-fly he was excited about. 'A real killer,' he said.

Later in the evening, Dr. Griffiths said: 'There was something I thought you might like to see. One of those little things that never came to be mentioned at the trial; and I only came upon it by chance.'

Vane felt a little uneasy as Dr. Griffiths leant forward, the desk drawer already pulled open. He rummaged around among the papers and odds and ends and held up an envelope, out of which he produced a cheque; with it there was a folded piece of paper.

'She always paid me every month,' he said. 'Put a cheque in the post for what she thought she owed me without ever waiting for the bill.' He gave a little shrug of his thick shoulders and squinted again at the cheque. 'She made a point of it.'

Vane didn't think of anything to say, he was too busy waiting for what was coming.

'She sent this the night before she died. Gave it to Nurse Howells to post.' Dr. Griffiths paused reflectively. 'She didn't want Merrill opening the envelope.' He handed Vane the folded piece of paper. 'You see, with the cheque was that.'

It was a letter scrawled all up on one side of the paper. She suspected her husband was in love with someone else, she wrote, but she had no idea who it was. Then she had realized that he was poisoning her. And now she was going to finish off the job he had started by taking a dose of arsenic which she had discovered her husband had hidden at the back of a cupboard just outside the bedroom.

Merrill's wife, Vane thought, his mouth suddenly dry, forcing herself to sit upright in her bed as she heard Merrill outside her door, coming in with her medicine. Forcing herself to compose her expression, while he stood in the doorway, smiling at her confidently, the medicine glass in his hand. She would smile back at him as she took it. She would drink it up, shutting her eyes, and opening them, find his gaze fixed on her attentively.

Her eyes would shift to a silver-framed calendar on the bedside table. 'Which reminds me,' she would say. 'I mustn't forget Dr. Griffiths's cheque.'

He would say something and as he went out of the room she would not see the expression on her husband's face.

And he would close the door quietly.

And he would not see her face.

The image faded from Vane's mind as he glanced round Dr. Griffiths's room, its old-fashioned, roll-topped desk littered with unanswered correspondence, a prescription pad, uncashed cheques mingled with bills, a dog-eared *Fisherman's Vade Mecum*, and angling catalogues.

He looked up from the letter. He could hear Dr.

Griffifths saying: 'How she got out of bed and to the cupboard is something I'll never know. Must have required a superhuman effort.' There was a little silence. Then: 'Was it because she didn't want to go on living, or because she wanted him to be shown up for what he was, her murderer? Or perhaps she thought I'd keep her secret; or just tell Merrill and no one else.'

'A woman who could do a thing like that,' Vane said, 'could have a dozen different ideas.'

'I can't help feeling there's something ironic that he was hanged for what he didn't actually do. We know that he would have done it, but the fact remains that she killed herself.'

Dr. Griffiths wanted to know was there anything he could do about it?

Vane said to him that there wasn't much he could do that would serve much purpose. It would only draw attention to him all over again. And for what? They were both dead, now.

Vane didn't know how he stemmed the compulsion again to blurt it all out, the same as he had nearly blurted it out to Merrill that time in the cell under the court. Vane wanted to scream it aloud how after he had left Margot Stone and found Davies, the idea had hit him. Davies had suddenly remembered about old Llewellyn having been Merrill's clerk, and how he had gone to live in Ireland.

Davies had the name of the village near Armagh, and Vane and he had made that night's boat to Dublin, and then driven like a bat out of hell. They arrived at the village, Davies had located Llewellyn and then Vane had driven them, pretending he was a hired driver, to Belfast in time to catch the plane.

When Philip Vane left Dr. Griffiths that night, he knew he would never come back to Castlebay. This new information completed the reason that he could never see Margot Stone again. He knew he would never be able to kill the terrible, tearing compulsion to tell her what he knew—and why he had done what he had done.

ABOUT THE AUTHOR
(1908-2006)

by Philip Harbottle

Born in July 1908 in Dudley, Worcestershire as Vivian Ernest Coltman-Allen, **Ernest Dudley** grew up in Cookham, Berkshire, where his father kept a hotel. Stanley Spencer lived next door, and was a friend of the family. Through Spencer's patrons, the hotel became a meeting place for artists and actors. Ivor Novello was a weekend fixture. The comedian and film star Jack Buchanan helped the young Ernest rehearse a song for an amateur concert.

At the age of seventeen Ernest left boarding school and joined a theatre company touring Shakespeare through provincial Ireland, in village halls and cowsheds. From this he graduated to the more upscale Charles Doran Company, and performed in proper theatres, paying its actors the munificent sum of £2 a week. For the rest of life he used and was known by his stage name of Ernest Dudley.

Always one with an eye for the ladies, Ernest soon met and teamed up with his late wife, the celebrated actress Jane Grahame.

Jane came from a theatrical family: her stepfather was Ellie Norwood, famous silent film actor who played Sherlock Holmes on stage. Through these family connections, Ernest secured work in the West End, appearing with Charles Laughton and Fay Compton, amongst others. When the original production of Noel Coward's *PRIVATE LIVES* transferred to Broadway, it was he and his wife who were recruited to take over the Laurence Olivier and Gertrude Lawrence roles in the British touring production.

His wife regularly played leading roles in the stage plays of Edgar Wallace, and Ernest would later create for her the character of Miss Frayle, assistant to Dr. Morelle in his radio plays. Other actresses would later take over the role. Most notably Sylvia Sims. Amongst the actors who played the good Doctor was Cecil Parker.

In the 1930s and 1940s he worked regularly for the BBC. In July 1942 his famous detective character (modelled on the autocratic film actor Eric von Stronheim, whom he had met in Paris in the 1930s) 'Dr. Morelle' made his radio debut on *MONDAY NIGHT AT EIGHT*. Dr. Morelle was a big hit with listeners, and engendered a long cycle of novels and short stories, a play and a film, and three series on radio. At around the same time, he launched another very successful radio programme, *THE ARMCHAIR DETECTIVE*, which ran for many years, and Ernest became known as "The BBC Armchair Detective." In this weekly programme he reviewed the best of the current releases of detective novels, dramatising a chapter from each. They included his dramatization of John Russell Fearn's 1947 novel *ONE REMAINED SEATED*, and it was this fact that would cause Fearn's biographer Philip Harbottle to seek Dudley out some fifty years later, to become his friend and agent. Notable amongst his many other radio credits is the fact that he was the first-ever radio jazz critic. In the 1950s he transferred to BBC television with an early audience participation programme, *Judge for Yourself.*

Back in the 1930s Ernest also ran a parallel career as a newspaper journalist, specialising and pioneering in show business gossip, working for a time with Val Guest, with whom he had also earlier worked as a film scriptwriter in the British "quota" studio system. Amongst his many newspaper 'scoops' was how he had collaborated with actor Fred Astaire in a London night-club on the creation of a new dance-step.

All of which only gives the bare bones of an amazing career as, variously, an actor, sports correspondent, jazz critic, playwright, novelist, gossip columnist, screenwriter and crime reporter. Most amazing is the fact that he became a marathon runner at an age when other people were drawing their pensions and relaxing by the fireside, and competed in several New York Marathons, writing a best selling book on how he achieved his amazing feats, *RUN FOR YOUR LIFE.*

Apart from some fourteen Dr. Morelle books, Ernest also published during his lifetime a dozen other detective novels, mostly notably *THE HARASSED HERO* (1951) which was subsequently filmed. He also appeared with short stories in leading detective periodicals such as *John Creasey Mystery Magazine* and, in the U.S.A., *Ellery Queen Mystery Magazine*. In the 1960s, and the following decades, he became established as the author of a long series of "animal" books for children, including *RANGI*, the story of a Highland rescue dog, and *RUFUS: THE STORY OF A FOX*. Ernest has also written novelisations of a number of films, along with a range of best-selling non-fiction books on diverse subjects, most notably *CHANCE AND THE FIRE HORSES* (Harvill Press, 1972) bringing to life Victorian London and telling the story of a dog, famous at the time, called Chance, who became attached to the fire brigade, and a favourite of the Prince of Wales.

An expert and enthusiast on the exploits of Sherlock Holmes because of his wife's family connections, Ernest wrote a two-act stage play, *THE RETURN OF SHERLOCK HOLMES*, which was successfully staged and taken on tour in 1993, with Michael Cashman as Holmes.

In 2002 a US publisher, Wildside Press, began to reprint some of his best detective novels, including a number of 'Dr. Morelle' adventures, in print on demand paperback format, available online. In 2005, the leading English publishers of 'large print' editions, F. A. Thorpe, began featuring Ernest's detective novels, in their Linford Mystery series, including the

'Dr. Morelle' books. All fourteen Morelle titles were quickly reprinted, followed by a number of new posthumous short story collections compiled by his friend and agent Philip Harbottle. These contained several unpublished Morelle short stories discovered in the author's effects, plus novelizations of radio and stage scripts.

Ernest continued writing right up to the end of his life. His last novelette, 'The Beetle', featuring Edgar Allan Poe's famous detective Auguste Dupin, was based on an earlier play broadcast on BBC radio, entitled *The Flies of Isis*. The new story was accepted for a Canadian anthology of Poe's 'Dupin' stories, alongside pastiche stories by John Dickson Carr and Charles Dickens. Ernest was checking the proofs in hospital at the time of his death. The anthology was fated not to appear, but 'The Beetle' has now been included in his new posthumous detective story collection, *DEPARTMENT OF SPOOKS*.

He is survived by his only daughter, Susan Dudley-Allen, a resident of New York in the U.S.A., who is devotedly overseeing the restoration of an amazing literary career.

www.ingramcontent.com/pod-product-compliance
Lightning Source LLC
Chambersburg PA
CBHW031427250626
47155CB00004B/1652